Chopping Wood, Shaping Metal & Other Erotic Stories

Chopping Wood, Shaping Metal & Other Erotic Stories

Lori Beth Bisbey

Dr Lori Beth Bisbey®

Dedication

For Morloki

with love & lust

Contents

| Introduction | 1 |
| Acknowledgements | 3 |

1.	Butch	5
2.	Shaping Metal	12
3.	Chopping Wood	22
4.	The Ticket	43
5.	Curls	51
6.	Sex Work	56
7.	Stalking 2020	61
8.	Dream Scape	96
9.	I Miss You	101
10.	On the Train	108
11.	Warm Morning	115

12.   Braids   *117*

13.   On Your Knees   *126*

14.   Edges   *131*

15.   Wings   *135*

16.   Epilogue   *138*

Other Books by the Author   *141*
About the Author   *142*

Introduction

Most of the erotica in this volume was written between May of 2020 and February of 2021. A few pieces are revisions of older pieces, ones written between 2000 and 2014.

As usual, some of the erotica is extreme. I write about the things that turn my lovers on, the things that turn me on. I write about BDSM, fetishes, and polyamory. I often write from my experience. When I am not writing from my experience, my characters inhabit my mind, my dreams and speak to me incesantly until I write them.

The work in this volume is made up of poetry, short prose, and short stories. One day I will turn one of these stories into a novel or compose a collection of short stories around one or two of my more insistent characters. That project will have to wait until I have completed the three other projects that are in progress.

If you want to understand more about my erotica, my Passion Map ^{tm}, please read my erotic memoir, Dancing the Edge to Surrender: An Erotic Memoir of Trauma and Survival. Otherwise, find yourself a private space, make yourself comfortable and come join me in my erotic world.

Acknowledgements

I continue to be blessed by a group of people who support and nourish me so that I have the energy to write.

My leather family, chosen family, bff's, son, and Masters – I love you all.

To my leather families (both) and the members of LHOCC:

If you think you see yourself in these pages, you are probably right....

And to those who are my special muses:

TJ Scott – husband, Master, best friend. You bring the spirit, fire, the water, the air, and ground me every day.

DK Green – Master – Your energy ignites. Your fire feeds. You bring balance.

For this collection, a variety of thirst traps on TikTok became muses. Thank you for the eye candy that fuelled my imagination.

Once again, thank you Meg-John Barker for mentoring this book to life. Your comments always help me to focus and encourage me to be my full authentic self in my writing.

Book Cover Design by The Book Cover Whisperer: ProfessionalBookCoverDesign.com

1

Butch

I see her as soon as I enter the play space. Her distressed leather trousers, white t-shirt with black harness, Sam Brown belt, leather motorcycle jacket slung over her shoulder. I look down and notice her boots could use some love and attention. By the time I reach her face again, her golden eyes are staring into me. She has a small smirk on her face. I immediately turn crimson. She nods in her direction as she walks over to the conversation area. She doesn't look to see if I will follow her, just knows that I will.

She pulls out a chair for me so I take a seat. 'Would you like a drink?', she asks. Her voice is honey and

smoke, a true contralto with a faint southern twang.
'Yes, please. A diet coke', I reply. She heads off to
the bar to get my drink. A couple of friends see me
and start to head over to talk with me. Before they
reach me, she returns. She hands me my drink and I
take a sip. She looks at my friends and they wave as
they walk by.

Her name is Kitha, she tells me. 'And you are known
as Jewel,' she says. 'Yes, I am, I reply. 'I noticed you
staring', she says. I blush crimson but stay quiet. 'I
am interested in you too', she says. My blush turns
even darker red. 'Here's what I would like to do with
you', she begins. My focus is on her lips, her eyes,
the contralto timbre of her voice. I have to work
hard to take in all her words. 'Does that appeal to
you?', she asks. 'Yes', I stammer. 'Is there anything
I should know about you?', she asks. 'Yes', I begin
and I detail my physical limitations, as well as my
relationship commitments. I finish by telling her that
she will need to talk with one of my Masters at least
and hand her my phone.

Both know where I am and I think Master Morloki
knows her – at least in passing. She certainly knows
that I am Morloki's Jewel and so she rings Master
Morloki. They talk for about 10 minutes as I sit

quietly, trying not to hear the conversation. My blush turns to a blood-red as I hear myself being discussed. This always highlights that I am a slave. There is always a hint of humiliation and a ton of heat associated with this kind of conversation. That I cannot consent to play with someone or have sex with someone as the agency lies with my Owners makes me so fucking hot.

They finish their call. Kitha takes my hand and leads me to one of the play stations that has a spanking bench with split legs so my body is supported and my legs are apart. 'I am not going to restrain you because I want you to hold your position. Is that clear girl?', she asks. 'Yes, Kitha', I reply. I am unsure as to what to call her so I choose to use her name. 'You may call me Papa' she says. I haven't called anyone Papa since 1984. It feels good to use the term again. It has its own flavour to it, different from Daddy or Papi. I reply, 'Yes, Papa'. She buries her hand in my curls and turns my head so that I am looking into her eyes. 'I like the sound of that on your tongue', she says and leans down to kiss me. She sucks my lower lip in between her teeth, her juicy lips. She nibbles then runs her tongue all around my mouth, exploring every part that she can reach with her tongue. I moan into her mouth and am breathless and dripping when she lets me go.

She starts with her claws – a set of silver steel, sharp as razors. She lightly scratches my back, my ass, my thighs. I struggle to stay still as I fear if I move, she will cut me. 'That's right girl don't move', she drawls. I cannot stop my trembling but I keep as still as I can. She digs into my ass with the claws and I yelp. She moves from claws to a flogger. It feels like it might be deerskin, soft, and not too heavy. She hits my back all over, my ass, and my thighs. By the time she finishes, my flesh is tenderised and I am oozing nectar all over the leather of the bench. When she hits my ass, my pussy presses into the leather. I want to come so badly but know better. She catches me, pressing myself into the leather, and flicks the flogger hitting me squarely on the pussy. 'Not until I tell you to come girl', she says. 'Yes Papa', I moan.

Kitha continues to flog me, changing from the deerskin to an elk which is heavier and rougher, and then finally to bull hide which lands with a heavy thud, almost knocking the wind out of me. I moan steadily. I can do nothing else but surrender to the sensations: the pain, the pleasure. Suddenly, I feel her hand between my thighs. She scoops up some of my nectar and brings her fingers to my lips. I suck them clean. She scoops up some more and then tastes me herself. 'Tastes good,' she hums as she slides two fingers into my pussy and starts to fuck me. She pushes in deep, hitting the G-spot, the A-spot, exploring every crevasse of my soaked cunt.

Kitha adds a third finger and starts using her thumb to rub over my clitoris. I am so close to coming. 'Please, please, please Papa please', I wail. 'Go ahead girl, come for me', she replies and pushes three fingers in as deep as they can go. I scream as my orgasm begins, the contractions holding her fingers tight, then releasing, and then grabbing again.

As the waves subside, Kitha says, 'I want to fuck you with my fist.' I shudder as I look at the size of her hands. She chuckles. 'Don't worry, I will go slowly and we will get there'. She adds some warm lube to my cunt even though I am dripping and then adds some to her hand. She takes her other hand and strokes my hair, gripping and pulling my curls lightly until I am purring with pleasure. 'That's a good girl. Relax. Open for me', she says.

Kitha slides two fingers inside my kitty and starts

stroking my G spot again. I move with her as she fucks me, moaning steadily by this time. She adds a third finger, then a fourth, still fucking me slowly. Finally, she pushes in with her thumb, curling her fingers slowly into a fist. The fullness, the stretching hurts but I want more. Behind the hurt is such intense pleasure I cannot describe it. It is the type of pleasure that takes away your power to speak, brings you to a primal space. As she fucks me, all I can do is accept what she is giving.

Kitha fucks me harder, faster and I can feel myself close to squirting. She can feel it too and encourages me to soak her. 'Just let it come, girl. Don't hold back.', she says. Her words draw the orgasm from me. I squirt soaking her hand, arm, and the floor. She slowly withdraws her soaked fist as I lay panting on the bench. She leaves me for a moment and comes back with towels and cleaning supplies to tidy up both of us and the station. Once we are clean and the area is clean and disinfected, she leads me off to a private room and has me lie down on the bed.

'Now it is my turn, she says as she straddles my chest and lowers her cunt onto my face. She smells luscious and tastes like smoky honey. I press my face into her folds and start worshipping her clitoris, her labia. Licking, sucking, nibbling on all parts of her amazing punani until she begins to moan and sits down hard on my face, forcing me into her. Kitha begins to ride my face, controlling my breathing as she does. I suck, lick furiously and then keep my tongue still as she rubs her clitoris on my tongue so that she gets just the right pressure in just the right spot. Her clitoris grows and hardens. I suck it into my mouth, licking around the glans, the head as I am sucking until she explodes. She floods my mouth with her smoky honey, almost choking me, covering my face with her sticky juice as well.

Kitha climbs off me, licks some of her juices off my face, and towels off the rest. She slides down next to me, wraps her arm around me, and pulls my head to her shoulder. 'Rest my good girl', she purrs in my ear. 'Yes Papa,' I reply as I begin to fall asleep in her arms.

2

Shaping Metal

I always look forward to the Ren Faire. I have been to a wide variety, including the original one at Agoura Hills, many times. I love all the entertainments, the noise, the bawdiness, the food, and the shopping stalls. The craftspeople who sell there are rarely the ones selling mass-produced goods. They sell goods made by their hands, in old ways, in family-run small businesses, preserving heritage often. Some of the skills are ones that are dying, like the traditional glass blowers. They have goods that you cannot get anywhere else.

This year, we go together. Master and I enjoying the opportunity to go explore a place together that we had explored so often separately. We are both amused that we missed meeting each other so many times more than 30 years ago. It is a sunny day so I take extra care with my sun protection and decide, in the end, to wear a hat as well even though I don't want to. Did I say that **I** decide? That should read, I obey as Master insists on a hat to protect me from the strong sun.

We arrive and start our walk around the Faire, enjoying the characters and the plays. We grab some lunch and start walking through the stalls. The glassblowers are fascinating. We watch them for quite a while. We stop at a stall with lots of leather clothing. I try on a skirt and top but don't end up buying them. We move on window shopping through the stalls until we reach the smith. He has a small forge and is working on a piece of metal when we arrive.

His muscles move under his skin as though they have a life of their own. They mesmerise me. I cannot look away. He has a head full of tousled dark brown hair. Tattoos move over his arms, shoulders, chest and they look alive.

Master stands behind me, arms around me as I watch. 'Are you enjoying the sight?', he whispers in my ear. I shiver, his breath hot in my ear, pushes the flames higher. His voice changes as we watch. I feel his shapeshifting behind me, arms gaining muscle and lengthening pulling me tighter into him. I recognise the form of Ogun and feel His amusement as I watch the smith pull the sword from the fire glowing yellow-orange. I cannot move my eyes away. My breath starts to come in pants as I feel each strike the smith makes. The strikes move through my whole body from my toes up through to the top of my head. Ogun chuckles in my ear and nudges me forward so I am in the shop, closer to the smith.

I am close enough to smell him now, and he smells like lightning and burnt earth. There is a musk that is so enticing I move forward without volition. Soon I am close enough to feel the heat from the forge. Behind me, Ogun pushes more and more heat into my body. Sweat beads on my face. As the smith shapes the metal, I feel his hands shaping me. My knees buckle. Ogun holds me up, whispering in my ear 'here is not the place to kneel girl'. I barely suppress a moan. The smith plunges the sword into water and I am doused with the cold as well.

The crowd thins out but I don't move. I watch intently, unable to move my eyes from the spectacle in front of me as the smith heats and shapes more metal and then dowses each piece in water. Ogun watches me as I watch. He pushes energy through me in time to the strikes of the smith's hammer. 'As he tempers and shapes steel, I temper and shape you', He says. I cannot speak but push my body back into his hands so he can feel my burning flesh. By the time the smith puts down his tools to take a break, my nectar is soaking my thighs and I am glad that I am wearing a dress with no panties.

He wipes his brow and removes the leather apron. He reveals a carpet of dark hair on his chest as well. It is contained by the tattoos. I lick my lips and he smiles. 'Hello' he says to us. 'Nice work', Ogun says. 'Thank You Master Smith', he replies. I startle, shocked that he recognises Ogun. 'This is my girl, Margalit', Ogun says. 'Pleased to meet you,' the smith replies. I blush a deep candy apple red. 'Pleased to meet you, Smith', I reply. 'Join me in my private space', he says as he leads us to a back area that is separated from the shop proper.

There are two chairs and a table. Ogun sits and I sink to my knees. The Smith grins. He takes out a horn and a bottle of mead. 'This is my special mead. Will You drink with me?', he asks Ogun. Ogun replies 'This body does not process alcohol well. But she will drink with you in my place.' He raises the horn to Ogun and takes a deep drink. When he passes the horn to me, he brushes my hands setting my body alight again. I drink deeply. The mead is special. It is sweet yet its flavour keeps changing. It starts with the honey, morphs to an effervescent berry taste, then deepens to caramel syrup, and finally finishes with a green herby taste. 'Thank you Smith. That is delicious.' I say. My head feels a little fuzzy. I adjust my position to be seated instead of on my knees so I don't fall over.

Ogun buries a hand in my hair as they are speaking, massaging my skull and setting me moaning. 'May

I?', the Smith asks. 'Yes,' Ogun replies and moves me between them. The Smith lifts my chin, looks at me for a long time. Then he says, 'I want to shape her through pain and pleasure. Mould her form for a while and command her responses.' Ogun just inclines his head. The Smith asks me 'Do you consent?'. 'Yes,' I reply quietly.

The Smith goes back into the shop proper to get supplies. When he returns, he has a leather-covered spanking bench and asks me to get up on it. 'Do I have to restrain you or will you be still for me without restraints?' he asks. 'She will be still without restraints', Ogun replies. I nod my head to assent.
I get up onto the bench and wait. I feel his hands on my body, shaping my body the same as his hands shaped the steel. Firm strokes make me moan with desire. It feels so good and all I want is to feel him inside me. I raise my bum to meet his hands. He laughs, a deep glorious laugh, and says 'Not yet girl. Not yet. First I must shape you and then temper you.' He continues roaming all over my body, bringing the heat, the fire to make my flesh malleable, and then shaping it as he sees fit.

He starts to pound on my flesh. It takes me a minute before I realise that he is using a small hammer, one of the tools he uses to shape iron, shape steel. He pounds my ass all around until it aches and burns. Next, he begins with a leather strap, one that he uses to sharpen edges. The first strike draws a scream from my lips. 'You must be quiet. Do I need to gag you?' he asks. 'no Smith.' I reply quietly.

The welts come up quickly with each strike of the strap. He pushes his energy through the strap, into my body, heating me further, shaping my flesh. He is skillful with the strap and lifts my ass with some strikes, catching that sweet spot on the underside but also the most painful spot on the top of the back of my thighs. He moves up my back as tears course down my face and drip onto the floor. I have managed not to scream by sheer force of will. I hear Ogun's happy sigh behind me. Feeling Him pull at the energy being poured into me. Feeling Him manipulate the energy, expand it and push it further inside me. I feel a glowing iron spike slowly push into me. Once inside it opens like a flower bloom, stretching me wide enough so it almost hurts. It pushes in deep, heating me from the inside, making me even more malleable for the smiths to shape. Ogun urges me to open, to surrender, and allow my form to be shaped.

'Be very still', the Smith says. The flames rise over

my thighs, my ass, my lower back. Once he has shaped me with the fire, it is time to temper me with cold water. He flows it over my body, quickly cooling me except for the superheated iron dick still pulsing inside me.

The Smith moves around in front of me. I can hear Ogun, at the table behind enjoying His tea. I can still feel the iron dick pulsing inside me. The Smith brings his hard thick dick to my mouth, rubs the head around my lips, wetting them with precum. My tongue snakes out to taste him as I moan. He thrusts and I suck his dick into my mouth and then my throat, taking as much of him as I can. His thickness stretches my mouth, and I can feel the corner of my lips crack. He thrusts harder, deeper – controlling my breathing. He tastes delicious. He thrusts in tandem with the superheated rod in my pussy, slow deliberate strokes, bringing me to the edge of orgasm and keeping me there. Each time I get close to the point of coming, he slows the pace. 'Soon you will be ready. Soon We will quench your thirst', he says.

The Smith buries his hands in my hair and holds my head to Him, filling my throat. He thrusts deeper, deeper. I can feel Him begin to pulse in my throat. 'Now, now come', he says as he comes down my throat. I feel the iron rod in my pussy pulsing in time and come moaning, struggling for breath, the energy tearing through me, moving to burn every cell and then bathe every cell with deliciousness.

The Smith slowly withdraws from my throat and I feel the iron rod withdraw slowly too. He helps me up and leads me to where Ogun still sits. I kneel and kiss Ogun's boots. He raises me up, smiling, and draws me in for a deep kiss. 'Good girl', he says, His pride in me evident in the timbre of His voice.

They help me back into my clothing and we exit the back room of the shop. The Smith asks us to wait for a few minutes. 'I have something for you', he says. We wander around the quiet shop looking at his work. He hands me a wrapped package. I open it to see the sword he had been working on when we arrived, the hilt wound in leather inscribed with Ogun's cauldron. I am in tears. 'Use it well. And come see me again', he says to us both.

We leave and walk back into the Faire, suddenly hungry, I turn to ask if we can go grab something to eat and see that Master has returned and Ogun has gone. He leads me towards the car park. 'Let's go get a sit-down dinner, maybe some Japanese?', he says. 'Yes, Master', I reply and we head back to town.

3

Chopping Wood

(With a nod to a number of TikTok Creators…)

The frost hits her face as soon as she leaves the car. Despite the mask, scarf, glasses and hood, the icy air penetrates right to her skin and beneath. She begins to shiver. Her thick coat and two layers are no longer warm enough. Her pace is slow as she walks against the wind through the trees to the cottage. It appears as though from a scene in a film – stone and wood built, smoke coming out of the chimney, snow on the low stone wall and the iron gate. Flashes of Hansel & Gretel run through her mind and she chuckles.

She brings very little with her for this stay. She plans

to spend most of her time in front of the fire writing and reading. She had the cottage stocked with food prior to her arrival. A few meals have been prepared and placed in the fridge ready for heating. There is a stockpot so a good thick soup will be her supper tonight. One of the owners is coming by in the late afternoon to chop some more wood so she has plenty for the fire. She hopes that she will be able to build decent fires as her husband usually does this job and she has never been very good at it. She can keep the fire going usually but starting it is not her strong suit. Maybe the owner will be willing to come by and start the fire when needed. She will ask him when she sees him later today.

She came upon this cottage by accident while trawling through the Airbnb listings. It was listed as an unusual one and the owners brothers, one of whom lived in the woods nearby. From their conversations, she ascertained he was somewhat of a recluse, living off the grid as much as possible and keeping himself off of his pension from a lucrative software development career, a few non-fiction how-to books that hit the best sellers and most recently a novel that had taken off. She discovered that he lived alone as he professed solo polyamory, meaning he has many partners but lives alone and sees his relationship with himself as his primary relationship. His voice was deep with a hint of sarcasm and had a peculiarly strong impact on her when they spoke. She has only seen a small headshot of him and noted his thick dark curly hair, 5 o'clock shadow, aristocratic cleft chin and thick juicy lips.

She shakes her head to clear it as she crosses the stone lintel and stamps her boots to get rid of the excess snow. She enters the room to a bright fire in the grate. There is a bottle of champagne, a crystal flute, a decanter of what looks like single malt and a squat crystal glass for the scotch. There is a bowl of fruit in the centre of the square old wood trestle table. She strips of her hood, scarf and coat, shakes them and hangs them on the rack by the door. She takes off the boots and leaves them on the mat to dry. She strips off the layers she put on against the cold and is left in her silk thermals and thick warm socks.

The room is lit mostly by the firelight the thick pile sheepskin rug in front of the fire looks inviting but she is aware that the wood floor is likely to feel unforgiving on her joints fairly quickly. She chooses instead to pour a glass of the whisky and sit down on the plush recliner settee and put her feet up as she recovers from the journey. She takes out her phone and connects to the WIFI as there is no phone signal here. She texts both of her loves to inform them of her safe arrival and clarifies rules for the trip away. She has been given significant freedom to choose what she does as far as contact with other people. This is to be a restorative trip and she plans to spend most of it writing, reading and walking in the trees. Eating good food will be a bonus.

Before leaving, she engaged in divination as she had been having strong flashes of intuition about the trip. The upshot of her work was an admonition to surrender to the moment while she was away. Surrender is a daily practice for her but surrendering to the moment remains a challenge. She was warned not to second guess herself. She was told to negotiate before the trip for all eventualities and made it clear to her people that this seemed to have a spiritual bent though for the life of her she could not figure out what sacred sexual experience she could be exploring in the middle of the woods in a cottage on her own. The pandemic meant she had missed most of her retreats in the 18 months, so she is just thrilled to have that freedom of alone time. She typically takes these retreats in California or Boston through to Maine in the US but the pandemic means that she has had to stay close to home again. The borders are open so she chose the wilds of Scotland as a location.

The Airbnb was not as expensive as it would normally be because of the pandemic. People are desperate to bring tourists back and revive their businesses. Her host did not survive on his Airbnb income. It was an adjunct, sort of like pin money – that bit extra that you save from the overall household budget, put aside for luxuries. Nonetheless, he made it more attractive because she was staying for at least 10 days, perhaps 2 weeks if she could swing it. She booked the two weeks with the understanding that she might have to leave after 10 days because he made the price sweet enough.

She comes to herself with a start. She almost drifted off. The fire is burning a bit low so she grabs a log and puts it on and prays for it to catch. She uses some artfully placed paper and it catches. She smiles to herself and then heads into the bedroom to unpack her clothes, change into a warm nightshirt and red cashmere robe, putting her feet into deep fluffy sheepskin slippers. She slides on her red cashmere fingerless gloves and lights the fire that was laid in the grate in the bedroom. It catches more quickly than she expects and she laughs at her good fortune. Once all her things are put where she wants them, she heads into the main room to start dinner.

She decides on a thick soup/stew of mutton, barley, carrots, onions, parsnips and sets to chopping the vegetables, browning the chunks of mutton and throws it all into the crockpot along with water, fresh rosemary, a little garlic, and sage. As everything is cooking, she takes the loaf of thick rye bread out and sets it on top of the Aga to warm. She sings as she works, enjoying the preparation of food in this spacious well-stocked kitchen.

While the food cooks, she sits down with a book and reads while sipping the scotch in front of the fire. An hour goes by and she hears a motor stop outside of the cottage. No one comes to the door. Shortly she hears the thwack sound of the axe splitting wood. At first, that sound makes her startle, but as it goes on it becomes a comforting rhythmic sound. She moves to the window and looks outside. Her host has stripped down to his t-shirt in the cold and his muscles ripple and bulge as he wields the axe almost over his head and brings it down with a satisfying whack, splitting the big log directly in two.

She begins to sweat watching him, watching the sweat start to soak his t-shirt as the axe rises over his shoulder and comes down again with another whack. She jumps this time even though she knows that it is coming. The more he chops, the more she feels like he is splitting her in two. Her hand snakes down between her legs to her very damp pussy. She parts her slick lips and begins to stroke her clitoris. She leans against the window frame to keep from falling. Whack…..whack……whack. He has built up a rhythm. His shirt is now soaked through. He strips it off in the now twilight. The dim orange and amber light sliding over his sweat dripping chest and back.

She groans audibly and strokes herself faster. She is so close that she can no longer keep her eyes open. Just as her orgasm begins, there is a knock at the door. She cannot stop the tide from overtaking her, moans and shivers as it does so he must knock again before she can bring herself to move towards the door.

She retrieves her robe, belts it loosely around her and lets him in. Her breathing is still ragged; she can barely speak. She motions with her arm to let him in. He looks at her with a slightly bewildered smile at her silence and ragged breathing. 'Are you

OK?' he asks, noting the red chest and cheeks and the glisten of sweat at her hairline, the smell of her pussy overpowering the smell of her very expensive perfume. He licks his lips and allows his grin to spread across his face. The dimples almost bring her to her knees. That mischievous smile is captivating. The energy building them between them is tangible – hot, thick, jagged in places.

She hasn't closed the door so he does it for her. He walks to the kitchen sink, runs the hot water, wets a hand towel and then rubs it over his face, arms and chest to wash some of the sweat away. She is still frozen, can only watch as the water droplets bead and run down his stomach. 'Oh. My. God.' she thinks as her gaze makes it down to his trousers and she notes the outline of a thick hard cock. 'Must say something or he will think I am dim or crazy' she thinks and struggles to speak. 'Would you like a shower?' she asks the blush deepening on her face until she is scarlet as she imagines herself on her knees in front of him in the large shower room, washing his feet, his legs and moving up his body…. She shakes her head to clear it and hears him chuckle. 'Thank you. I think I just might have one. I will see you shortly' he says and he heads off to the shower.

His voice is sublime. It is far deeper than she expected and the Scottish brogue is delicious. She has to pay attention in order to hear his words because the lilt draws her in and she finds herself listening to the music of his voice and missing the meaning.

She sets the table for two as the stew is finished. She makes a salad while she waits for him to exit the shower. He comes out and notes the place settings at the table with a raised eyebrow. 'My supper is just ready. Would you like to join me? Chopping wood is hungry work.' I ask, inwardly cringing at the sound of my own words. The slow smile crosses his face again. 'Yes I would love to' he replies.

Eventually, she relaxes into dinner, enjoying the food, drink and conversation. The last of the sun disappears while they eat. He takes his time eating. She enjoys watching him. Every so often, she slips off into fantasy, imagining his lips on hers, his tongue, his teeth. A couple of times she has to suppress a moan and blushes beet red. He doesn't ask, just grins and continues to eat.

The meal finished, she clears the table. 'Would you like coffee, tea, a nightcap? And there is some cherry pie for dessert', she says. 'Black coffee and I would love a piece of pie', he replies. She sets the coffee brewing, the reassuring drip reminds her of home. She busies herself tidying the kitchen while waiting for the coffee to finish. She can feel his eyes on her, keeping her blush alive.

She brings him a large mug of coffee, a piece of warm cherry pie with a dollop of fresh whipped cream. She takes a mug for herself and a small piece of pie and joins him at the table. They eat quietly. 'This is good pie', he says. 'Thanks. I love baking when I have the opportunity,' she replies. He continues to stare at her and smiles as her blush becomes scarlet again under his gaze. 'Let's move to the settee' he says. Before he settles down with her, he goes outside and gathers some of the wood. 'Looks like it might snow', he says as he comes in with the wood and sets to building up the fire again. The glow on his bare chest almost makes her drool.

He comes to the settee and settles next to her. This close, his musk is overwhelming and she doesn't manage to fully suppress a groan. Now her face is vermillion. 'Is something wrong?', he asks, the Glaswegian lilt filled with humour. 'Not wrong,' she stammers. 'You smell..' He doesn't let her finish the sentence, rather draws her into a kiss. He takes her lips, devouring them, pushing his tongue between her teeth. She opens to him and feels him pouring into her. His energy is dark yet sweet, intoxicating, enticing. She feels him moving through her body until he is filling every available molecule. She hasn't even the will to kiss him back. All she can do is surrender.

The kiss seems endless. His hands move to her face as he adjusts the angle of her head. She has a fleeting thought, 'This is one of those movie moments I always find so hot' before pulling herself back into the present.

He presses his thumb up into the flesh under her jaw causing her to gasp. He sucks on her tongue, chews on it until she feels a bit of pain but not enough that she would want to pull away. Her nipples tighten as she moans into his mouth. She opens her eyes and he is staring straight into her. His eyes dance with amusement.

'Shall we get more comfortable, lass?' he says as he leads her towards the bedroom. The four-poster bed was one of the selling points of this cottage even though she thought she would be spending the time alone. He helps her out of her robe, takes off her nightshirt. She is a curvy girl yet he lifts her as though she were insubstantial, made only of air. He places her in the centre of the bed on her back, then spreads her legs wide and moves her arms up over her head. He is still in his jeans.

He moves to a wardrobe and pulls a key out of his pocket. It's an old-fashioned skeleton key and he has to jiggle it in the lock. He reaches inside and grabs a handful of lengths of blood-red silk. He deposits the pile on the bed next to her and then brings out a half dozen red and black pillar candles. He places these around the room and lights them, the golden flickering glow all that illuminates the space apart from the moonlight streaming through the window. She notices that the curtains remain open and then silently chides herself. There is no one within miles of this cottage to see her nakedness.

'I would like to make full use of this bed and tie you to the posts. Your safe word is red. Say yellow if you need me to back off. Otherwise, I assume you are enjoying yourself. Do you understand?'

'Yes ....' she almost sighs.

'Good. You may call me Maestro. Do you have any questions?'

'No Maestro'.

'Do you consent to surrender to me for this time?'

'Yes Maestro'

And with that, he ties her feet to the bottom two posts, and her arms to the top two. He stands next to the bed and slowly strips off his jeans. He is commando and his half-hard cock springs to attention. She groans as he starts to slowly stroke himself.

'Can you see girl?', he says. She can only moan. 'Let me get a little closer', he says as he climbs on top of her, straddling her chest with his glorious ass resting on her tits. She watches in awe as his girth increases. He is above average in length but not frighteningly large. His girth though looks to be well above average.

His chest beads with sweat again so his musk permeates the room. She is enveloped in his scent, wants to taste him so badly. A few minutes of stroking and he moves up to her face so his balls are over her mouth. 'Open', he instructs. She opens her mouth wide as he lowers his balls to her lips. Her tongue flicks out over his balls and she is rewarded with his first groan. She lips his balls, exploring running her tongue between around, sucking his sack in her mouth, nibbling as she sucks until he rasps out a sharp 'Stop!'.

She does as she is told, chuffed to hear him panting above her. He leans over her and rubs his cock around her face, pressing into her cheeks, over her lips, into her hair. He grasps a handful of soft curls and wraps them around his dick, groaning again as he begins to stroke. He strokes harder, faster, his sweat landing on her face. She wishes desperately that she had her hands free so she could stroke her kitty in rhythm with his thrusts. She salivates at the thought and almost drools.

Suddenly he stops stroking above her. With effort, he moves off her face and chest and lies down next to her. He runs his thumb around her lips and presses on them until she opens her mouth. He strokes her tongue until she starts sucking, licking his thumb. She feels the pull of heat energy from deep in her vagina up through to her mouth. She feels as though she were going from solid to liquid when heated just like coconut oil.

He removes his thumb and runs his fingers and then his tongue to her neck where he sucks, bites and then bites just a bit harder. His teeth are sharp and she is sure he will draw blood. She can't decide if she craves this or it terrifies her. He doesn't draw blood, just moves lower to her nipples and begins to suckle in earnest. The energy intensifies and the pull becomes stronger. Her moaning becomes plaintive cries as she crashes into orgasm. He continues to suckle as she recovers, past the point when it begins to feel 'too much' but she stays with it.

He moves down her body, licking, sucking, nibbling until he reaches her mons. He starts to nibble around the top and down her outer lips, licking up the nectar that is gathering there. She moans, thrusting her hips up, wanting more contact with his mouth, lips, tongue, teeth. 'Do you want something?' he says and she can hear the humour in his deep lilting voice. 'Yes Maestro. Please', she gasps. He stops. 'Ask for what you want', he says, the humour gone from his voice. 'Your lips, your tongue, your mouth on my pussy, my clit. Please. Maestro', she stammers, still not good at voicing her desires clearly.

Seconds pass into a minute as he looks at her. Time stretches until he finally runs his tongue over her clitoris. She screams with pleasure. He sets to tasting her – sucking, licking, nibbling as she moans, cries, screams in pleasure. Her orgasm is quick and hard. He laps up her juices and slides two fingers inside her pulsating pussy, quickly finding the G spot and setting up the finger pattern that is bound to make her squirt.

She doesn't like to squirt until she actually does it. The getting there feels too intense. She hates the stimulation of the urethra so that she feels like she needs to pee even though she knows she doesn't. She could call red but doesn't really want to. This is one of those love-hate things. She has a number of those when it comes to sex and especially kink and BDSM.

He drums on her g-spot, fucks a rhythm that makes her hoarse from screaming. When she is close, he can feel it and he can feel her holding back. 'Let go for me, lassie. Open to me', he says and she feels something shift inside of her and then the orgasm overtakes her, like a tsunami. She soaks his face, his arm, the sheets and he roars in triumph. Without allowing her to rest, he slides up her body and buries his cock deep in her cunt. He stretches her so that the penetration is just a bit painful. She is still restrained making meeting his thrusts impossible. All she can do is receive what he chooses to give.

He fucks her faster, harder, increasing tempo until she knows he is ever so close to coming and stops when he is at the edge. Pulling out of her, he slides up her body, straddling her chest again and wraps his pulsating dick in her hair. He groans as he slides into her silken curls. The silk and slight abrasiveness of the hair adding to the increased arousal as he objectifies her. He takes only seconds to erupt, spurts of hot come soaking her hair.

He runs a come soaked finger over her lips and she sucks it greedily into her ravenous mouth. His taste intense smoky and sweet. He strokes her face, slowly climbs off her and heads to the loo to clean up. She can hear him singing softly as he towels off.

He comes back to the bed and asks 'Do ya need to use the loo lass?'. 'Yes, Maestro', she says. He releases her and she sits up slowly. He rubs the feeling back into her limbs and she yelps in pain. She heads to the loo, debates showering and washing her hair when she hears him at the door. 'Not yet. I am not finished with you,' he says softly but firmly. She comes back to the bedroom.

'Up on the bed' he says. She complies. He is quickly atop her and slaps her across the face. Tears spring to her eyes from the pain and the shock. He traces his fingerprints as a slow smile spreads across his face. His cock is already hard again and pulsing. He reads the question in her eyes, 'Because I want to. There is no other reason', he says. One tear rolls down her cheek. He tastes it and sighs in pleasure.

'On your knees, lass', he says. He positions her with a bolster under her to lift her ass high. He pushes cold lubed fingers into her ass. He rubs his dick around her asshole. She breathes deeply, willing herself to relax. The more relaxed she is, the more likely it is that she will enjoy this, if he lets her. He strokes slowly into her ass. His girth makes this far more difficult than she expects. The stretch hurts burns as she tries to adjust. After a few minutes, the pleasure begins alongside the pain. She moans as he presses into her. It feels as though she will split in two. Her moans become screams as she gets closer to orgasm. 'That's right, lass. Open more for me,' he rasps. She breathes deep and wills her body to let him in further. He picks up his pace, still stroking fully – all the way in, as deep as he can go and then out except for the thick head of his dick. She wishes she could stroke her clit as he begins to pound into her. All she can do is ride the wave with him. He pours energy into her with each thrust that rushes through her body bringing every nerve ending alive, causing her to feel he is fucking ever single atom of her being. She feels her orgasm begin as she moans 'please please please' but she does not know what she is begging for. The first orgasm gives way to a second and then a third in quick succession as he comes deep inside her ass.

He collapses on top of her, nibbles on her ear until his breathing slows down a bit and starts to approach normal. She goes to move and he holds her down, growling in her ear. She is perfectly still as he bites the back of her neck, growling as he chews. There is a direct connection from his teeth to her pussy, juice overflowing. She rubs her pussy into the bolster beneath her, desperately trying to push herself into another orgasm. 'Stop that, lass', he growls. She wails in protest but stops.

After a while, he rolls off of her and leads her to the shower. He takes his time washing her body, her hair and especially her kitty until she is purring, so close but he will not yet let her come again. She washes him thoroughly. He dries her with lots of big fluffy towels, wraps her in a robe and leads her into the lounge, to the sheepskin rug before the fire. She lies down as he busies himself in the kitchen, bringing back two hot whisky drinks and some biscuits as refreshment. She is quiet as they eat and drink, feeling off-balance but happy.

'A penny for yer thoughts, lass?', he asks. 'I am not really thinking. Just feeling, Maestro' she replies. 'You need some rest or you will not get anything done. I will tuck you in and be back tomorrow to check the fires, and chop some more wood', he says, a chuckle evident in his voice. 'Your will, Maestro', she replies as she yawns. He picks her up, carries her to bed and tucks her under the big, sumptuous duvet. He kisses her on her forehead and then again traces the finger marks still lingering on her face. 'Goodnight lass', he says. 'Goodnight, Maestro.' She replies. She is asleep before he makes it out of the cottage.

4

The Ticket

'Oh fuck, damn shit!' I shout as I stub my toe on the raised nail for the fourth time that day. I am late for a meeting and likely now late for the whole day. Days that have me at more than one location are always the most challenging. I find it difficult to figure out what to wear and what to bring with me. I envy those women who seem to find it easy to bring one or two accessories that make their outfits go from day to night with ease and always know how to artfully change their makeup to look smashing after being on their feet for 12 hours already.

I have on a wrap mini dress made of deep plum silk. It clings to my bare thighs and the push-up bra gives me enviable cleavage. I can't find the matching pants so I am commando today. I complete the outfit with deep purple leather Dr Martens. They are butter smooth to the touch. I spray on Enslaved by Roja Dove, one of my favourite perfumes rich with carnation, oakmoss, vanilla, and ambergris. I coat my lips in a deep berry gloss.

I rush out the door, jump into the car, and set out for my first meeting. It's a 15-mile drive and if the freeway is traffic-free, I will only be 5 to 10 minutes late. Two miles into the journey, there is a traffic jam. I work at my breathing, trying hard not to lose my cool. I hate being late. It always makes me feel off balance. The traffic unsnarls and I step on the accelerator to try to make up the time.

I love my car. It is so responsive it can be hard to keep track of speed. I am focusing on making up time, thinking about what I will need to do after the meeting, and don't realise my speed has crept up to 80 mph until I hear the sirens behind me. 'Fuck, shit, shit' I scream to myself as I pull over to the shoulder. I don't have time for the traffic stop and this ticket is going to be expensive.

I am digging in my bag for my license and

registration as the officer comes to the window. The tan hat and mirrored sunglasses make it difficult for me to see his face. I roll down the window. 'Do you realise how fast you were going Ma'am?' he asks me. 'I'm sorry Sir. I am late and I guess the speed got away from me.' I reply. After a moment, I realise that he is staring at my tits, my thighs. I spread my thighs just a little wider.

'License and registration Ma'am' he says but his voice is thick with lust. I hand over the paperwork and his hand lingers on mine. He returns to his vehicle to check the documents and my insurance. I watch in the mirror as he walks away. He has a gorgeous, high round tight ass. I can feel my juices start to drip on my thighs. My nipples tighten.

He comes back to my window. 'Ma'am, I need you

to follow me'. He says. This makes me nervous. 'Do you want this ticket? Or...' he says. 'Yes, Sir. I will follow you'. He leads me off the next exit and to a small motel. He parks around the back at room 103. I park next to him. He opens the door to my car and escorts me into a small immaculately clean room. He takes off his hat and reveals a beautiful smooth bald head, deep umber eyes, a luscious moustache over full lips, and a blindingly bright smile.

He pulls me towards him and leans in for a kiss. I melt as he begins to slowly explore my lips. He slides his tongue around them and then between them and tastes my tongue. I moan as he explores further, licking at the roof of my mouth, between my lips and teeth, sucking on my tongue gently, chewing my lower lip until my knees buckle and he is holding me up.

The meeting forgotten, I sink to my knees in front of him. He undoes his belt and the sound is enough to cause me to moan. The shhht as his zipper lowers starts me drooling. He lowers his trousers and his black cotton briefs. His cock springs out almost fully hard. He sits down on the bed as I move between his knees.

I lower my head to his beautiful thick long cock and begin to explore. I start at his balls, licking and lifting them with my tongue. Sucking as much of them into my mouth as I can. He groans as I explore and begins to stroke his cock slowly. I move up his delicious tool until I reach the frenulum, licking, tasting, inhaling his musk. Finally, I reach the head. He is cut so nothing is hidden. His head is swollen and pulsing as I slowly suck him into my mouth. The feel of him in my mouth is divine.

I start to suck his cock as though my life depends upon it. I worship his dick as he slides further into my mouth and into my throat. He is content to let me have control as I do this, allowing me to control the pace and depth for a while. As I suck, lick, I slide my finger behind his balls to massage his perineum. He moans as I put pressure there. I slide my finger back and run it along his asshole without penetrating. He buries his hands in my curls and takes back control.

Now he controls the depth and the pacing as he plunges into my throat. He moves faster and faster. One hand reaches down to squeeze my nipples until I yelp around his dick as he pounds into my throat. Suddenly he stops. 'I want your tongue in my ass' he rasps out as he pulls his cock out of my throat.

He slides up on the bed, lies on his stomach and spreads his thighs. I slide between them, grabbing his gorgeous ass cheeks and spreading them. I plunge my tongue deep into his asshole and he groans. As I lick and suck his asshole, my hand moves between my thighs. My fingers rub my clitoris frantically as I push my tongue as deeply into his asshole as I can. I am seconds away from an intense orgasm when he tells me to stop.

'I want to fuck your face' he says. He puts me on my back on the bed and straddles my face. He slides his dick back into my mouth and begins to fuck my face fast and hard. My hand is back between my legs, rubbing my clitoris. My clitoris is hard and slippery between my fingers as he strokes himself into my throat. I can feel him pulsing. He picks up the pace and I know he is close to coming in my mouth.

He winds a hand in my hair and holds my head onto his dick as his orgasm begins. His deep bass moan as he fills my throat with ambrosia is enough to push me over the edge. I come bucking underneath him. He slowly pulls out of my throat and squeezes the last few drops of come onto my lips and tongue. Then he climbs off of me and goes to the bathroom to wash off the sweat before redressing. I wonder if I have done enough to avoid the $300 ticket.

He comes back into the room to dress and I dash into the bathroom to try to clean up so I look presentable for the rest of my day. I walk naked back into the room. He stares at me as I cross to grab my bra and dress. 'You have just paid your fine Ma'am. Please watch your speed' he says with a grin on his face. 'Thank you officer I reply as I put on my dress and fluff my hair. He hugs me and slides his hand between my thighs, slipping a finger into my still sopping kitty. 'I would love to spend some time getting to know you better' he says as he starts stroking my clit until I am purring again. 'I am going to give you my card. I hope you call.' He says. He kisses me before I can reply and doesn't stop until I am breathless. When he lets me go, I say 'Yes Sir Officer, I would like that'.

We leave the room and he locks up. I wonder how many women he brings here each day. He gets back into his patrol car and I get back into my car. I have completely missed the first meeting and am already late for the second one. His last words to me are 'Drive carefully, Ma'am'. said with a chuckle. I laugh and drive off, being careful of my speed.

5

Curls

As I slowly pull the brush through my thick curls, I reminisce. My hands become Master's hands, pulling firmly but gently, working out the knots. As the tangles come free from my hair, the tangles inside me work loose. Sitting between his legs, aware of his heat. The tension between relaxation and arousal, pulling like the snarls at the base of my skull. I breathe in the scent of him mixed with the scent of my hair released with each stroke. The smell of my scalp mixed with my hair, body oils, perfume, smoke from the fire burning in the room.

My breasts are full and sore, the ropes of blue-green veins pulse across them. I feel my blood move through them, hot viscous, salty, sweet, tang. His hands are massaging my scalp now and then pulling through my hair. I smell the oil as he opens the vial – sandalwood and olive, a touch of vetiver and coconut. He drips it onto my head slowly. One drop at a time, they run into my scalp, drip onto my forehead and down my face, fall onto my shoulders, onto my back. Slowly dripping my breathing is synchronised with the dripping.

Master's hands work the oil from my too dry scalp to the ends of my hair. There is a frisson of electricity and then a spark as he touches me again, dragging a moan from my chest. He pulls me to him and works on my shoulders with his solid hands as the oil does its work. My muscles liquefy and I can barely rise as he pulls me up to lead me to the shower.

I stand quietly as he lathers my hair, rinses it, and then applies the first of the conditioners. I moan as he washes my body with the peppermint shower gel, tingling everywhere his fingers touch. I moan as the water sluices over me, washing away the soap and the first conditioner. And then again as he works the second conditioner into my hair – scalp to tips. I stand with eyes closed, leaning against him under the hot spray as the conditioner fortifies my hair.

Master shocks me awake biting into my shoulder, orgasm taking me without warning, juice squirting from me, mingling with the hot shower spray. He chuckles and washes the last of the conditioner away.

He takes me out of the shower. His fingers penetrate my ass and pussy as he dries me, as if doing so by accident. I fold into him further. I am dizzy as he rubs the rough towel over my hair.

Master applies the after creams and unguents to my hair and body and leads me to bed. His fingers trail over my breasts. I lean against him with my still wet hair free. We drift together as my hair dries.

My hair is soft and full, thick curls resting on his chest. He gathers a handful of my hair, pulling my head back until he can claim a kiss from me, invading my mouth, almost pressing into my throat until I again liquefy.

My curls cling to his fingers, creating a floss cage. He presses his hand against my scalp, spreading his fingers and gripping again, tugging at the roots and then tugging at the shaft as I sigh with pleasure. He sets up a rhythm of tugs and pulls and my pleasure builds until I am emitting a steady purr. The purr becomes a groan as his nails scratch at my scalp and his fingers dig in at the dip right at the base of my skull.

He drags his fingers from their silken trap and takes another handful of curls, pulling my head into his chest and then pushing me down toward his half-hard dick. I breathe him in until my nose is at the root, buried in his tight kinky curls.

Now my ringlets become the way he controls his thrusts and the way I can tell when he begins to lose control. He pulls, pushes, directs my mouth, lips, and tongue using my curls as a joystick, a lever. His hands completely entangled now as he thrusts until he pushes through the tightness at the back of my throat until I relax and let him slide all the way down. His hands in my curls control my breathing now – throat convulsing around his sword. As he picks up speed, his hands clench and unclench creating a maze of soft springs. He tastes of salt sweat & a hint of zest from when he fucked me earlier today. I work on him sucking, licking as his hands in my corkscrews control the pace.

My world narrows until there is nothing but his fists in my locks, his cock in my pulsing in my raw throat, and the puddle of oil dripping from my snatch. The sound of his groan when I slide my finger into his tight tropical butt brings me closer to my own orgasm. I try to quicken the pace so he will permit me release but his hands hold me in place as he begins to piston in and out of my raw mouth and throat.

Quick breaths are all he gives me as he moves towards his peak. His moan is steady as I suck harder, turning to a groan and then a howl as he fills my throat with his thick salty seed. I work at the root of him to get every drop. I am suspended on the edge of my own orgasm as he pumps into my throat. His hands stay tangled deep in my curls as he says 'come'. My orgasm starts at my toes and moves up enervating my nerves, muscles, skin, releasing fluid from my core. My pleasure suffuses through my curls, loosened, more relaxed in the afterglow.

6

Sex Work

Cindy and I met at work. She is local and has a broad
North Shore accent. She chews gum incessantly.
Her clothes are too tight, showing off every bit of
her body. When she wears jeans, there is a distinct
camel toe and I cannot help but stare. I try to imagine
what she would taste like. She flirts with me and
loves it when I blush. I have little experience with
women at this point, but I want to taste her so badly.
There is something I find so enticing about her. She
is downright nasty. I have always had a thing for the
nasty, that rough edge. Up until now, I have never
acted on it.

One day we are in the loo and she calls me into her

stall. She grabs me, shuts the door, and kisses me. She tastes of cheap wine and cigarettes and smells of smoke, cheap perfume, and sex. I swoon. My knees become jelly as she explores my mouth with her teeth and tongue. 'You like to be told what to do, don't you?', she asks with a smirk on her face. 'Yes', I stammer. 'Good' she says as she lifts her top and bares her tits. They are large melons with big pale pink nipples and a smattering of light freckles. The nipples fill my mouth. I suck in deep, running my tongue around the tip and then the whole of the nipple.

Cindy shoves as much of her breast in my mouth as she can, forcing me to open as wide as I can. 'I'd love to choke you with my tit.', she rasps. Abruptly, she pulls her tit out of my mouth and presses me to my knees. 'Suck my cunt' she says, her voice rough with desire. I reach out tentatively and she pulls my head forward – pushing my face into her hot wet folds. Her rough hair tickles my face. Her cunt hair holds the scent of sex and the scent of her piss and breathing her in makes my cunt pulse and drip.

I lick her cunt, find her clitoris and suck hard, rhythmically. She comes quickly, bathing my face in her juice. She holds my head to her and starts to piss.

I swallow quickly. She tastes strong and nasty but I come almost immediately. 'Oh. You like that? You disgusting, nasty girl. I can make money off of you. You want to earn some easy money? Sure you do. Clean up and make yourself pretty', she says. I wash off in the sink and she helps me to apply lipstick.

Cindy brings me to the place where she occasionally turns tricks. She puts me in a room and tells me to strip and wait. She comes back into the room with the first man. '$50 for a blow job with you shooting on her face', she says. 'How much to piss in her mouth?', he asks. '$50', she says as she holds out her hand. She takes the money from him.

Cindy sucks on his dick until he is ready to shoot. He stands in front of me pulling on his dick. 'I'm going to mess up that pretty face. Open your mouth', he says. I open my mouth as the first shot of sticky spunk hits my cheek. His moans when he comes are high pitched almost yips and I giggle. I realise my mistake as the rage crosses his face. He moves towards me to slap me and Cindy gets in the middle. 'That will cost extra', she says. He grumbles and hands Cindy a crumpled-up $20 bill. She moves aside and he slaps me across the face. Tears spring to my eyes and tumble down my cheeks. I try not to whimper.

'Open your mouth whore', he growls. He pisses in my mouth. Cindy is watching and rubbing her cunt. 'That's so hot.', she says. 'Come here now and lick my cunt', she demands. I crawl to her and start licking.

'I want your tongue in my asshole', she says. Before I can do anything. Two other men approach. 'We are going to put on a show – lie down and wait', she says and heads to the next room. When she returns, there are 5 more men with her. 'Money first', she says to the men. All of them are in work clothes and most smell like they have spent the first part of the evening drinking in the local bar. Cindy gathers the money and puts it in her bra.

Cindy lifts her skirt and sits on my face. 'Stick your tongue in my ass', she says. The men are in a circle watching, all pulling on their dicks. My tongue is in her ass and she farts and then laughs. It is disgusting but my pussy drips and my clit pulses. My hand moves between my legs and I start rubbing my clit. Cindy moves so I can lick her cunt, suck and lick her clit. She comes hard and squirts in my mouth, over my face and chin. She pisses down my throat and quickly gets up to leave my face free for the men to wank over. All of them are close to coming and cover me in spunk quickly. My face and hair are covered. Two of the guys wrap my hair around their dicks and use my hair to finish off. The party ends with two men trying to piss the come off my face.

I have come 6 times during this party and am exhausted. Cindy takes me into the bathroom to clean up. She kisses me and tells me how much fun she had and then hands me $200 which she says is my share of the take. I get home and fall into a deep sleep almost immediately.

7

Stalking 2020

The house is dark and somewhat cold when I startle awake. I take a few minutes before getting out of bed. I cannot figure out what woke me. I get out of bed and wrap my red cashmere robe tightly around me. I slowly walk through the house and out the back door into the garden. I shine my torch around but all I see are the sleeping chickens in their run. I walk up the garden to the outbuildings but no one is there. The hair on my body is standing up. Goosebumps appear on my arms, legs, and across my chest. I walk quickly back to the house, close and lock the door. I walk round the house checking all the windows and doors, unlocking and relocking them, walking the perimeter as I used to do when the PTSD was strongest. One circuit, two, three. I stop myself and put myself back in bed. I turn on the television, strip off my robe, and then slide between the sheets. Eventually, I fall into a fitful sleep.

The morning is cold and grey. I dress warmly in black jeans, deep red cashmere jumper, leather coat, leather gloves. I wind a colourful scarf around my head and neck. Sliding into my red doc martens, I grab my mask, sanitiser, bag and keys and I'm off into town. There is freezing fog making the drive to the station treacherous. It looks beautiful hanging over the fields. I get to the station car park and find a space. I'm heading into London to meet Tai for lunch and a bit of shopping. We haven't seen each other for a while with the pandemic and I am looking forward to hearing all about her new love.

Shopping since the pandemic has changed drastically. I still have not adjusted to the new normal. I have only been once since March and that was fun but an extremely strange experience.

I head into the station and get my ticket. Down on the platform, the hair raises on my body again. I feel eyes on the back of my neck. I turn quickly to try to see who is watching me but I see no one there. I am unnerved. 'Breathe' I think and slowly count my breaths, in for five beats, out for five beats until my pulse returns to normal and the hair on my body settles. I look around the platform at the people awaiting this train. We are all spread out, avoiding each other for fear of catching the plague. This is my first train journey since March 2020 and I almost decided to drive in.

I catch a glimpse of someone in a leather jacket and jeans. There are two women whose bags I covet. Another woman whose dress I covet. And a third women who I simply desire. She is lush – full breasts, round ass, and a medium waist with thick black hair bound into a long braid. Her coffee skin lightly freckled and her hazel eyes sparkling. She meets my eyes, grins and I blush, realising I have been staring. The train arrives.

I take a seat in the first-class carriage. The train is so empty. I have never been on a close to rush hour train where people weren't in all the seats and standing next to me. The lush woman sits in the next allowed seat. I can smell her perfume, wood mixed with spice, and a tuberose top note. She is intoxicating. She smiles at me and goes back to reading her book. I find it difficult to concentrate and spend the rest of the ride enjoying her, feeling her heat, and inhaling her scent. She gets off the train at London Bridge, slipping her card into my bag as she leaves and blowing me a kiss. I flush a claret-red. On her card she has written 'Call me, lovely.' Her scent lingers on the card.

I get off the train still thinking about the luscious woman and wondering if I will have the courage to call. I walk out of the station heading towards the taxi rank. I see a driver in full livery holding up a sign with my name on it. Surprised, I wonder when Tai organised this and how long the driver had been waiting. I am distracted and don't pay too much attention to the driver. He opens the door for me and I thank him and climb into the car, enjoying the smell of the leather seats. I get comfortable, lean back, and close my eyes and he starts to drive. The driver turns the music up, an eclectic mix of stalking music. I lean back and close my eyes. I fall asleep as we drive through London. I awake with a start when the car stops. It is then I notice how dark the windows are and how little I can see out. The driver opens the door and helps me out of the car. We have arrived at a large Victorian home. I am confused but before

I can ask any questions. The driver returns to his car and drives away.

The hair on my body has risen again. All of my senses are on edge as I walk up the three stairs to the front door. I lift the great brass knocker in the shape of a lion's head. The door opens slowly, creaking like in an old horror movie. I walk in tentatively. 'Hello' I say, feeling as though I am in a low-budget film. I walk 50 more yards and hear the door slam behind me. I jump and I hear a chuckle. I look towards the sound but don't see anyone.

I enter an old-fashioned library. Beautiful solid oak shelves filled with books – hardbound, leather-bound, softcover. Some are clearly very old and others modern. There are library steps. I am in seventh heaven. I love libraries and I love library steps. The smell is of old leather, slightly musty, and fine cigars. There are two overstuffed blood-red leather chairs, each with an ottoman in front. The reading lamps are old-style banker's lamps. There is an open fireplace on the south wall, emanating a comforting heat. There is no one in the room. I begin to look at the books. The first one I pull out is a first edition hardcover copy of 9 ½ weeks. The next, a leather-bound illustrated edition of The Story of O. I look more closely at these shelves. There is erotica of every genre from every era. 'Mama Vi would love this place' I muse as I continue to examine the collection. I become so engrossed in exploring, I forget to wonder why I am here. I am in the midst of reading one of Xan West's stories when I feel breath on my neck. I startle dropping the book and turn quickly around.

You smile at my jumpiness. 'Anxious?' you ask quietly. 'What am I doing here?' I reply, unwilling to admit anxiety at this stage. 'Answer me' you say. 'Yes. I am anxious' I say with a strident tone wondering why I am answering you at all. I did not ask to be brought here. I'm supposed to be having a girl's afternoon with Tai. I am in a strange home, with an intensely hot butch invading my personal space. My stomach is turning. My hands are shaking. My mouth has gone dry and my cunt is soaked. The hair continues to stand on my body. My initial response is primal – fight or flight and I am desperate to flee. The moment before the adrenalin fully kicks in, is a moment in which I am frozen to the spot.

You walk slowly around me, taking your time to look at me. The first circle allows me a modicum of personal space. The second time around you are closer and by the third circle, you are damn near on top of me. I can feel your eyes holding me as though I were one of those butterflies, pinned into a young boy's collection.

'Strip' you command. I am about to argue when I feel the look in your eyes, daring me to do just that. Instead, I slowly remove my clothing. I am not trying to be sensual as I am much too anxious, but somehow, taking my time, it becomes a sensuous strip. I turn my back to you as I remove my jumper and my trousers. I turn back to face you and kick off my boots. I slowly remove my bra and finally my pants. You remain impassive, though I can feel the heat coming off you in waves. My breathing is shallow, my pulse racing. As I stare at you, a challenging look in my eyes, my mind is screaming 'wrong! Don't challenge! Show deference!'. A tremor runs through my body but I continue to meet your gaze. After some minutes, I lower my eyes. You chuckle.

As you examine me, I feel as though someone is pushing down on my shoulders until I slide to my knees. I am surprised to find myself there, kneeling at your feet. You press your foot in between my thighs and spread them wider. A gasp escapes my lips. You continue to walk around me. The first strike comes as a complete shock. You leave a handprint on my face. The sound like a crack of thunder in my ears. The second strike comes quickly on the heels of the first, slapping my head back, leaving the imprint of your fingers on the other side of my face. I remain on my knees shocked.

Your boots appear before my face again. You press my head to your boots. I know what you expect. I kiss your boots. What starts as a perfunctory act, becomes an act performed with desire and devotion. An unexpected act of worship. You move to one of the chairs and settle into it. I stay with my head to the floor. I hear the rustle and clink of chains. Tremors move through my body but I do not move.

I remember being in the woods with Stuart when I was 12. He had a net he used to catch butterflies and sometimes dragonflies. Sometimes he would chase them and swoop down with his net, snaring the creature. He would examine what he caught and if it was an 'interesting specimen' he would put it in a jar to take home and pin into his collection. If it was not of interest, he would unwind the net and tap it until the insect flew free. Other times, Stuart would stand stock still and hold out his net. He would wait for the butterflies or dragonflies to enter the net and then quickly trap them. Still, other times he would walk quietly, stalking the flying beauties until he was close enough to pounce. Stuart took me home with him to show me his collection. His eyes lit up as he spoke about the collection. His cheeks turned pink and he would lick his lips. His excitement animated his whole body. I remember feeling weak and dizzy as I looked at the collection, the insects pinned in neat rows. When I went home that night, I rubbed myself off to thoughts of being stalked and caught just like those butterflies.

Here, in this room, I am caught in your net. I wonder if I will be thought an interesting specimen and you will want to keep me or if I will be found unworthy and set free.

I hear you rise. You walk around me again, taking in the measure of my breathing, the trickle of sweat between my shoulder blades, the tremor that moves through my flesh as you get closer. I wonder how it was that I missed the net. My hypervigilance usually serves me. This time, it only served to confuse. Too much information meant that I missed the more subtle clues. After all, butterfly nets are sheer and can be difficult to see.

Your hands on my left ankle bring me quickly to awareness. The steel ring is cold and heavy. The chain attached to it sturdy though not too unwieldy. The steel of the wrist restraints is frigid and I wonder where you have been keeping them. You bind my wrists together in front of me, allowing about a foot of chain in between so I can manoeuvre a bit. The tremors through my body are stronger. My nipples have turned into rubies – hard and deep red. My cunt continues to drip. I alternate between burning and freezing, my temperature illustrated in the colour change that moves over my body. You are standing back in front of me. My face is still to the floor. Those damn boots are in my face again and I cannot resist the urge to cover them with kisses. I'm sure I have never done this before and watch myself in awe, wondering what the hell has come over me. I'm caught and I cannot figure out how that happened. I feel vulnerable and raw, and desperate for release.

You raise my head and look into my eyes. I kiss your hands as they pass my lips. I couldn't speak if you asked me to at this moment. All words have left me. My hunger consumes me. I am panting, breasts quivering with each short breath. As you watch my nipples tighten again until they are sharp ruby points.

Standing in front of me, the outline of your cock is eye level. Gods, I want to suck you so badly but I cannot even speak. You have my hair and pull my face to you. Your trousers against my face are rough and comforting in their roughness. I can smell your arousal through your trousers and I moan with need. You let go of my hair and move to sit on the chair again. The chain pulls as you step back, the sound of the links musical. As you pull the chain towards you I have no choice but to crawl towards you. I whimper as I crawl more from the humiliation than from any pain. You are watching me carefully. Your gaze singes my skin and burns through to my soul.

'There are some rules' you say. 'We will go over them. When I finish, you will have a choice. Leave or consent to do as I say. You will only be asked once.' 'Yes Sir' I whisper. You are talking about respect and deference, taking care with how I speak, how I look, looking to your needs, always considering what you might want before making choices. Valuing my mind and skills as tools you can use. Part of me is shouting 'No. I am independent. I will remain independent' while the rest of me feels as though I can finally let out the breath I have been holding in for years. I can breathe. As long as I follow your rules I will be able to breathe and feel. When you finish you simply say 'Choose'. I lift my head, clearly looking in your eyes, and say softly but clearly 'I wish to stay'. I have taken in a deep breath. I hold it while you consider what I have said. Praying that I will be found worthy. You smile. 'Good girl' you say as you stand up. You bend me over the leather ottoman, secure the ankle chain to the heavy oversized floor lamp in the corner. You leave my hands secured together.

You leave the room. I am plunged into terror. I do not know who else is here. I do not know fully where I am. I fear the silence in the room. I fear who else will be here and who might see me in this condition, naked and bound to an ottoman. I wait quietly, breathing to try to control my fear. I have goosebumps all over my body.

Suddenly, there is music. It is dark with a penetrating beat. The acoustics in the room cause it to sound like it comes from a cavern. It arises out of the air. I always find that disconcerting. The first strike of the crop catches my left ass cheek, slightly off centre. I groan softly. The second strike lands right next to the first. The next few strikes continue the line down my ass cheek. They land quickly and with medium force. I yelp and as you continue to strike my ass, my thighs, I moan. I lose count before you stop. My body is covered in a sheen of sweat. I pant quick shallow breaths.

You are in front of me, undoing the bindings securing me to the ottoman. 'Turn over' you rasp. I comply and you bind me on my back over the ottoman. You place my head on a couple of big firm pillows to give me some support. I am still somewhat bent so not able to truly watch you except when you are behind my head. The first strike of the dragon tail lands on my belly. I squeal at the sting and the heat. You begin slowly, striking with precision my breasts, my belly, and then my inner thighs. Wildfire spreads over my body as the strikes build upon each other. Tears stream down my face as you hit harder and faster. You abandon the dragon tail for your hands – slapping, hitting, and pinching. This is harder to manage without sobbing. You hit faster and harder, smacking my pussy now until I am wailing. The pressure is intense. I burn Gods I burn. I want you to stop. I want you to keep going. I want. I just want. Gods. I beg with seemingly no volition. The words being dragged from my core. 'Please please oh, Sir please please' 'Please what girl? What do you need?' I can hear the passion in your voice. 'Please Sir please let me come please.' I cry. The fire has reached my chest and is moving up my back. Soon it will completely engulf me. I am suspended in this moment of need knowing that it belongs to you, just as all moments belong to you. You bite my breast, gnawing on that vein that crosses above my nipple. 'Now. Cum now.' you command and continue to gnaw on my breasts as the flames engulf me, my orgasm burning, melting until I disappear – form dissolving in the flames.

You gnaw, chew, suck at my breasts, marking them clearly. You bite down my belly, leaving a string of marks. You bite on my mons until I screech. I want to push up into your mouth and I want to pull away all at the same time. You bite in that junction between thigh and cunt. That sweet spot which will continue to remind me for weeks after of your pleasure. Bites there linger and the pain lingers far longer than bites in some other places.

You remove the bonds, chaining my hands together in front of me. You grab my head and pull it towards your dick. I open my mouth wide, determined to take as much of you as I can. I wonder if this is your biggest dick or if I will have to learn to take even more. I hope it is the biggest as I am having trouble swallowing you. You push back into my throat. I suck hard, running my tongue where I can until you take full control of the pace. You will take what you want. You are fucking my throat, fast and hard almost to the point of completely controlling my breathing. I struggle to avoid choking. Your hands are in my hair, pulling as you push into my throat. Tears leak from my eyes as you pound into my throat. I want so bad to feel you cum as you fuck my throat. You fuck me faster, hands tangled in my hair, moving my head where you want it. You pull me to you grinding into my throat, groaning as you cum. Tears course down my cheeks as you pull out of my throat. All that can be heard in the room is our ragged breathing.

You stretch out on the plush carpet on your back, pulling my head to your chest and we lie quietly while you stroke my hair. No thought, no analysis – pure contentment. I am centred in the moment, knowing I am where I am meant to be at this precise point in time.

I wake up with a start, having drifted off. I am alone,

hands free, ankle still chained to the large heavy floor lamp. I sit up slowly, listening for clues as to where you might be. I am hungry, thirsty and I need to pee. I get up and start to explore the lengths of my chain. There are two doors in this library. One on the east, I came in. The second on the north side of the room. My chain is long enough to reach the north doorway. I walk slowly, trying to work the stiffness out of my muscles and get the measure of the chain. The sound of the links tinkling and dragging along the floor makes me shiver. I open the door and move out into the ornate hall. I reach the first door and discover it is a bathroom. I sigh in relief that I will be able to relieve myself without asking for permission. I would find it so embarrassing to have to ask but more than that, having to wait when I really need to pee is really difficult.

I get into the bathroom but realise that I cannot completely shut the door on the chain. My cheeks turn pink that I can be heard and that anyone can walk in. Sweet relief to be able to pee. I wash my hands and face, use a finger to brush my teeth with some toothpaste I find. I cannot get into the shower still chained so I simply top and tail with a washcloth.

When I walk out of the loo, I feel refreshed. My chain is almost at its limit so I return to the library.

I return to the shelves and find the book I was reading. You arrive to find me in one of the leather armchairs, reading erotica. I look up as you approach. You are almost silent on your feet but the air crackles around you. The energy in the room shifts. It feels as though a storm is coming. I can almost smell the thunder and lightning. Should I stay in the chair or sink to my knees? The bolshie girl in me wants to stay where I am but the slave at my core needs to sink to my knees. I am on my knees by the time you reach the chair. I bend to kiss your feet. You let me stay there, head to your feet, for what seems an eternity and in reality is only a minute or so. You lift my head, thumb on my carotid, stroking as you examine my expression.

'Are you hungry?' you ask. 'Yes Sir' I reply. You open the chain and take it off the lamp, wrapping the loose end around your fist. 'On your knees then' you say. The look of terror on my face makes you chuckle. You don't have to ask twice. I drop to my hands and knees and follow you as you lead me to the kitchen. You help me rise and show me round this large country kitchen. The larder is fully stocked.

'This morning, I will cook. You can tidy up after.' you say and then chain me to the table leg. 'Sit comfortably' you say as you begin to create breakfast. The sizzle and scent of the bacon draws a moan from my throat. It has been sometimes since I was treated to crisp bacon. My mouth floods with saliva. I watch as you take berries out of the fridge and chop them. I shiver at the sound of the knife on the cutting board. You look up, capturing me all over again. The butterflies in my stomach overtake me and I am trembling, the links of the chain betraying my state.

The food is ready and the smells remind me that I am ravenous. 'I am going to let you feed yourself' you say and I find myself pouting. You don't invite me to move however and place my plate on the floor next to me, along with silverware and a cloth napkin. I wait until you nod at me and then dig in. The food is divine. The bacon is perfectly crisp and full of flavour. The pancakes are golden brown, loaded with berries and the taste of the pure Canadian maple syrup is the perfect compliment. Bacon grease lands on my chest. As I go to wipe it off, you stay my hand. 'I will get to that' you say, setting me trembling. Syrup lands on my nipple. This time I simply leave it. We finish eating. I rise to take our plates to the kitchen and to begin clean up. You pull me to you, slowly licking the bacon and syrup from my breast, your teeth scraping my nipple. I moan, my knees beginning to buckle. You bite down and begin to suck. My moan turns to wordless pleading. My own syrup heating and running to soak my pussy lips. You feel the scar tissue from my healed piercing. 'I bet the nipple piercings looked good'. 'Yes Sir' I reply. 'Why are they gone?' you ask. 'They didn't settle well'. I reply. 'Hmm.' you grunt and I am unsure what to make of that sound.

You let me go and I set to cleaning the kitchen and putting everything away. I feel you watching me as I work and I am more clumsy than I would like. I manage not to break anything and finish. I come out of the kitchen and kneel at your feet. You take me through to the playroom. The room is fully kitted out with a range of bondage and whipping furniture. My eyes widen as I note the range of torture implements on the wall. 'Go get the tool you wish to be beaten with and bring it back to me' you order. I panic, the butterflies spinning in my stomach. I realise if I wait too long, it will be worse and I make myself move. I cross the floor slowly. Do I choose something that I like? Do I choose something I believe you will like? Do I choose something that fills me with fear and desire? I run my hands over the various crops. I move on to the quirt and the cat, shivering as I touch them. I can feel your eyes burning into my back as you watch me move around the room.

I get to the paddles and tremors run through my body. Then the straps – the smell of the leather makes my knees weak. There is a selection of sjamboks next. Now my knees buckle. I pick up a black one of medium thickness, running it through my hands. I take it with me to the next display: two dragon's tails, a signal whip, and a leather tawse. I pick up the purple dragon's tail and bring it with me. I come back to the centre of the room and kneel at your feet, offering you the sjambok and the dragon's tail. The tremors run through my body so strongly I fear I will break apart.

You help me up onto a spanking horse. You are about to secure my arms and legs with straps. You pause 'Can you lie still without being restrained?' you ask. I bite my lower lip and then say 'Yes Sir. I think so'. You arrange my limbs as you wish saying 'Don't move'.

I become aware of the music for the first time, the insistent rhythm pounding in my blood. You start with the sjambok, the first strikes landing on the centre of my ass and causing me to scream. I manage to stay in position, breathing hard. My instinct is to run. I override this and stay still. The next five blows land on my thighs, each one welting and bruising. I begin to sob. The sjambok is a wicked evil torture instrument and wielded by someone with your power and sadistic glee, it is most diabolical.

The strikes fall on my back now – knocking the wind out of me. Tears cover my cheeks and begin to drip off my nose. I am wailing as you begin to strike the backs of my arms. The tip of the Sjambok cuts. You move to strike my calves and then the bottom of my feet. I am struggling desperately to stay in position for you. The pain is excruciating and has not yet morphed to the pain that gets me high. I am enduring, holding tight to my agreement with you. Just when I think I can stand no more, you stop beating me. You move in between my legs, running your hands over the welts and bruises, scratching them, pinching them, tapping on them. Each time you cause a fresh rush of tears. Your hands on my ass make me shudder. You reach between my legs, scoop up some of the thick sap that has collected in my pussy. You feed me my own juice while I moan around your fingers.

You step back. 'Turn over' you say, your voice velvet over steel. I am face up now, legs spread, cunt exposed. You pick up the dragon tail watching while I shudder. The first touch of the tail is on my inner thigh, a quick sting and then a scrape. The second on the other thigh, causes me to jump. 'Don't move' you warn. A flick of the tail lands on my mons. A rain of hail lands on my outer pussy lips. Lashes land on my stomach, welting with little spots of blood immediately. The expression on your face is one of pure delight. You pepper my breasts with welts, blood drops now instead of spots.

You start striking with more power – whipping my thighs, my tits until I am sobbing. Then somewhere as the blows fall, the pain turns and I am moaning.

As you strike my nipples, I hear myself begging. 'Please please please Sir please fuck please Sir. Please, Gods I need please.' You are between my legs, flicking the tip of the tail on my pussy lips. 'Please fuck me please Sir.' You press your dick slowly into my sopping cunt. My hips rise to meet you and you shake your head no. 'Don't move' you warn. I struggle to stay still as you stroke into me. First short teasing strokes, then deep strokes – pounding into my cervix. You pinch my left nipple between your fingers and squeeze as you fuck me – watching the flush rise over my chest. 'What do you need slut?' you ask as you keep pounding my pussy. 'Please Sir I need to cum Sir please' I wail. 'Cum then' you reply. I cum, screaming with release, trying ever so hard not to move. You continue to pound into me, chasing your own orgasm. 'You can move' you bite out. I move to meet each thrust, legs wrapped round you until you can lean down and bite my chest as you find your release.

You pull slowly from my molten core, sweat dripping on my chest. So completely sexy. I cannot stop watching you. You catch my gaze and watch the new blush rise, chuckling.

'Off to the showers' you say, leading me out and into the large wet room. The room is the size of a typical British double bedroom. There is a claw-footed tub for two. Half the room houses a shower with two showerheads and multiple shower jets. When they are all turned on, the sensation is that of being surrounded by pounding water, an upright whirlpool bath. There are heated towel racks and huge soft plush towels. There is a door to an attached room that houses an adjustable massage bed. It is oval-shaped, 4 ½ feet wide and 6 feet long. 'Sir, would you like a massage?' 'Yes girl'. 'I will start on your front first' I say and help you to lie down on your back. I switch on a relaxation mix and peruse the oils in the bamboo cabinet. There are a few massage oil bases: jojoba, rapeseed, arnica, almond, and calendula. These are arranged in 4 oz bottles. I choose the arnica for sore and tired muscles. There are over 100 essential oils in quarter dram bottles to add to the bases. I choose vetiver and lime for relaxation with a boost.

I begin with your feet, working oil into the soles. Massaging the soles, the tops, each toe using medium to deep pressure. I move to your calves, working out the knots as I go. On to your quads, working to get in deep. You groan as I work the sore spots. I move to your stomach, clockwise circles, and then on to your chest. Working the oil into your pecs, using the palms of my hands first and then my fingers to work more deeply. I have entered fully into the massage – strong fluid motions, my body weight working to add strength. I work down each arm. Spending extra time on sore biceps and triceps. I work your shoulders and the back of your neck from the front, slowly until you finally begin to loosen. I move to your face and head. The oil now warm smells heady mixed with your own scent.

I spend a long time on your head, until I can feel you begin to drift. I don't want to disturb you, but it is time to work on your back. 'Sir' I whisper in your ear 'It is time to turn over'. It takes a moment until you register the meaning of the words I am saying. You turn slowly, placing your face in the hole, allowing the padding around your head to support your weight. I move to work on the back of your neck. I work carefully and thoroughly, isolating each knot. You groan 'good' as I keep working. I move and begin to work the trapezius muscle where so much stress is stored. I spend a long time until I finally feel it release. I move further down your back, taking my time, muscle by muscle.

When I get to your ass, I groan as I work the oil into both cheeks. I'm not sure I can keep from drooling, my cunt is dripping, nipples tight and raw. I refocus and continue to work until I feel the muscles release. I move to the hamstrings and then to your calves, finishing with your feet. By the time I am done, you are almost asleep. I dim the lights even further and sit down at the foot of the couch. The chain clinks lightly as I work to get comfortable. We both relish the time to rest.

After a while, you wake, gather up the chain, and gently shake me. 'Time to get up' you say. I open my eyes, stretch and then slowly rise. You lead me on the chain into the shower room and start it going. The steam begins to fill the room as we both walk in. We are both tired, take time to wash thoroughly, and enjoy the jets. The silence is delectable. You pull me to you and begin to wash my hair. You take time to massage my head as you lather my hair. I moan with pleasure as work the conditioner into the roots. You hold my head back, palm on my forehead so that the conditioner stays away from my eyes. The water flowing over me and down my back is exquisite. We wrap up in warm fluffy towels and leave the bathroom. During this whole time, the chain has not left my leg. I am sure I would feel strange without its weight.

I have lost all track of time outside this house. Aware that my stomach is empty, I ask 'Sir, would you like me to fix you something to eat?' 'Yes, slut.' you reply and lead me back to the kitchen. 'What do you fancy, Sir? I ask and you laugh at my choice of phrase. 'Surprise me' you reply which sets me to trembling. I look in the extra-large fridge, assessing the provisions. I stick my head in the larder to see what else you stock. I am torn between adventurous and comfort food. Having looked through the provisions, I choose comfort food and set to making lasagne. As the ground steak is browning in the pan, I prepare you some coffee and offer it to you from my knees. You take it, stroking my hair briefly. I head back into the kitchen and continue the cooking while you relax with your coffee. After 20 minutes, the lasagne goes into the oven for final cooking. I tidy up the kitchen while the lasagne is baking. The smell of the roast garlic, tomato, and cheese is enticing. I come to sit at your feet during the last 10 minutes of cooking.

I head to the kitchen to dish up the food. 'Fix two plates' you say. 'Yes Sir'. I load the plates with lasagne, garlic bread, and salad. I bring them to the table and then return to pour you a drink – single malt with a jug of water on the side. 'Pour one for yourself' you command. 'Thank you, Sir'. I bring the drinks to table and stand awaiting your word. You seat me opposite you and then begin eating. The food is tasty and filling. We say little as we eat. I don't realise the extent of my hunger until I begin to eat and it is not long before I have cleared my plate. When you have finished, I take the plates to the kitchen and place them in the dishwasher. I put the finishing touches on the strawberry shortcake I have made and bring the cake and knife to the table. There is a bowl of melted chocolate to use for topping. You cut us each a piece and drizzle the chocolate over the top. The confection is divine, causing me to sigh with pleasure. You retire to the lounge with a cigar and your scotch. When I finish tidying up, I move to sit at your feet. We watch the sprites in the fire as it crackles. Sometime later you announce it is time for bed.

You attach the chain to the post of the bed. I climb into bed next to you and work hard to settle to sleep. Before I know it, I have drifted off.

I wake on my own, still chained to this bed. My muscles are sore, pussy aching. I stretch for a few minutes and then head off to the bathroom. Having completed my ablutions, I set out to see what the length of this chain is now. I pass two rooms and am standing looking at the art on the wall when you catch me. Arm around my throat, pulling me backwards and quickly putting the hood over my head. I scream. I cannot help it. I am petrified of hoods. 'Quiet' you whisper and I am left whimpering.

The hood is thick, soft leather – elk maybe. The smell of the leather is earthy and somewhat intoxicating. The hood dampens sound as well as smell and, of course, totally obscures sight. I continue to whimper, my whole body shaking. "Don't panic" you say quietly, your arm still round my throat. 'Panicking will only cause you to hurt yourself'. 'Yes Sir' I say but my voice sounds muffled and full of fear. I tell myself to breathe slowly, in for 5 breaths and out for 5 breaths.

Your arm tightens around my throat, cutting off my breathing for seconds that feel like minutes. A gush of nectar runs onto my thighs. I hear you chuckle but only barely. You let me go suddenly and lead me down the hall.

'Walk carefully' you say. 'There are four steps down, then a landing 10 steps across. Then another three steps down. When you reach the bottom, the post is five steps in front of you. Go kneel there and await me'. I want to protest, to tell you I cannot do this.

Instead, I say 'Yes Sir' and slowly begin to make my way down the steps. I reach the landing without falling. I feel a breeze on my naked body, raising goosebumps on my skin. I reach up with my hands and touch the hood – feeling the butter-soft leather under my fingers. I feel the chain around my neck and the lock that keeps the hood on. I slowly move forward and almost fall down the second set of stairs when I lose count of my steps. I catch my balance back, however, and just land a bit hard on my feet when I reach the bottom stair. I walk slowly to the post, thick as an old oak tree. It is thick enough that I cannot get my arms around it. I kneel at the foot and wait.

I do not know how much time you leave me here to wait and whether or not you can see me as I do. I experience waves of emotions while I wait. I start with simple fear which morphs into panic and then to terror. There are no thoughts that go with these emotions. They are a response to being hooded. I experience excitement and arousal, also a response to being hooded. I can hear nothing from outside this space. I can smell nothing from outside this space. I feel the air on my skin, keeping the goosebumps alive.

After an eternity or perhaps only a few minutes, you

say 'rise'. I stand and you turn me to face the pole. 'I am going to beat you. You are going to count out the strikes. If you lose count, I will start again. I am going to give you 100 lashes. You will thank me for each one and ask for the next one. This will allow you a small amount of control of the pace so that you can keep your breath. Should I feel you are abusing this privilege, I will simply deliver the strokes at the pace I choose so beware of counting too slowly or too quickly. Do you understand?' you ask. 'Yes Sir' I reply, and my voice cracks as I do. It would be hard enough to manage 100 lashes with whatever instrument you choose had I my vision, my clear hearing, and a clear sense of smell. To do so while hooded is petrifying as none of the things I almost unconsciously do to manage a beating of this intensity are at my disposal. Somehow, being able to discover what I tool is being used, helps me cope. Stripped of some of my coping strategies highlights the myriad ways in which I am out of control.

The first lash surprises me. It feels like you are using a belt. I count '1 thank you, Sir. Another please' with little pause between my thanks and my asking for the next. Strikes 2 through 10 land on my ass as horizontal stripes. You are hitting me about once per second. I jump with each strike. Tears begin to fill my eyes. Strikes 11 through 20 land on the back of my thighs as horizontal stripes. You are still hitting me about once per second. The pain has caused the release of endorphins and I am a bit high. My adrenalin levels are still very high and the combination is exquisite.

You turn me round on the pole. Lashes 21 – 40 fall at one per half-second, starting at my chest, over my tits, and then down my thighs to my knees. Again you lay these as horizontal stripes. I am now finding it difficult to manage the pain. I scream the count, my thanks, and my request for the next strike. You spread my legs by kicking them apart. Lashes 41 to 50 land on my inner thighs. I wail as I feel the bite of the leather, knowing the welt will rise and swell and that it will be hard to put my legs together for at least a week. These welts you layer on top of each other. I take a couple of seconds during this series to ask for the next strike, sobbing and finding it hard to catch my breath.

'51. Thank you Sir! oh please I can't. Next one please Sir' I wail, beginning to dance from foot to foot. This strike cuts into the sensitive flesh at the top of my left inner thigh, where my tattooed braid winds round my leg. It feels as though you have drawn blood. 52 lands at the same depth, same intensity on my right thigh. For 53 to 60, you alternate between thighs, kicking my legs apart further as I try to close them. Growling at me to open my legs and endure. After strike 60, you run your hands over my body, squeezing the welted flesh, feeling the burning heat, gathering up drops of blood on your fingers. The relative gentleness of your touch causes me to sob anew.

You turn me back to face the pole. Lashes 61 through 80 land at one per every two seconds. You use the dragon's tail to lash across my back from my shoulders, down over my ass to my thighs and wind up with three on my calves. The dragon's tail lands on top of the welts from the belt, opening some of them up, making some of them swell and abrades the others. My knees begin to buckle but I hold to the pole. Coldwater hits my back causing me to scream. I feel the rivulets run down my body. 'Only 20 more slut. You can do it.' you say quietly. 'Yes Sir' I moan.

You turn me round so my back is to the pole again. 81 to 95 – the dragon's tail lands on my breasts and renders my nipples bright red and raw. The dragon's tail rakes across my thighs. I am shrieking. My clit is throbbing. 'You can choose where the last 5 strikes will land. I will hit you even harder than I have so far. Choose now' you demand. '96 on my left breast, 97 on my right breast, 98 on my left inner thigh, 99 on my right inner thigh, and 100 on my mons please Sir' I say, voicing shaking but clear. 'Good' you reply. The last five strokes are harder than the previous ones. My voice is raw from screaming. I collapse onto the pole after the final lash. You quickly release me so my full weight does not stay on my wrists. You lower me gently to the ground. Everywhere your hands touch my body, everywhere my body touches the ground hurts. I wince as you move your hands over my welts, examining all the places where my skin has broken and blood oozes or runs from the cuts. Deftly you clean each cut, causing new pain as the antiseptic does its work. You slather antibiotic cream over my body. When you are finished, you gently remove the hood. My face is soaked from my tears, my eyes swollen and puffy. My lips are raw. You kiss me, biting at my lips until they are swollen. You take my breath. I shudder in your arms. 'Now you look completely ravaged' you say. 'Thank you, Sir' is all I can say.

After a time, you help me upstairs, wrap a light silk blanket around me, placing me on a plush sofa. You come sit with me, stroking me absently while you watch the fire.

8

Dream Scape

I lean down and rub my ankle as I get ready to teach my workshop. The soreness radiates into my calf, a dull pain that leaves me wanting more as I rub. Just as I wonder where this soreness is from, I think 'Well I was chained last night'. I startle, the dream image sharp in my mind. My knees protest as well. I remember kneeling before you, my hunger hitting so quickly that it knocks my breath from me.

That charged languor returns to me and I am enveloped in the energy. I can barely keep my eyes open as I sink deeper. I am naked but for collar and chains, on my knees in front of you. My body is covered with a sheen of light sweat, juices thick and slick between my thighs. My fragrance is heavy and sweet – shades of frankincense and amber from Roja Dove's Enslaved parfum overlaid on my sweat and juices. The air around us crackles with the energy we exchange though to anyone looking on, we appear to be doing very little. Time takes on that elastic quality I love so much when in ritual space and slows. Down. Until. There. Are. Many. Beats. Between. Breaths.

You inspect me, observe me as you pull energy from me, push your energy into me and the feedback loop takes on another curve. My colour rises and I moan – a deep raw sound starting beneath my toes where my soul is embedded in the earth and rising to my groin bubbling in my pussy, my ass and swirling up to my solar plexus where an incandescent sun begins to burn moving to my heart, landing in my throat opening me further and then bursting from my mouth. I vibrate with hunger, so much so that I am salivating and close to drooling, blushing a deep crimson as I feel the liquid collect in my mouth.

'Sit comfortably' you say and I move to take the pressure from my knees. I notice the cold shackle around my ankle and the links of chain leading to your hands. As you move the chain back and forth between your hands, the sound has me mesmerised. 'What shall we do today?' you muse though I know this to be a rhetorical question. You will do what you will at any given moment and I will surrender. You pull me towards you until I am between your legs and you can get a hand in my hair, pulling firmly until I am looking at you. I lose control, body trembling, ever so close to coming from the energy play, the connection.

'What are you thinking?' you ask. 'Edges. I am dreaming of edges. Blades, blood, ritual markings.' I whisper. I see a fire, a ritual blade, hear the drums. Goosebumps rise on my naked skin. I feel the heavy silk velvet of the blindfold as you tie it round my head. 'Don't move' you say. I stand still but for the trembling as the cold of the blade touches my skin. I am only aware of the sensations, my feelings. The soft grass and crisp leaves under my feet. You lead me to the stone altar. Sit me up on the slab. 'Lie back' and I do so slowly now aware of the cold stone beneath me and the chill air above, the heat from the flames seems farther away.

I hear your chant, the words of the ritual are not intelligible now though we went through them this was agreed. I feel the flame run over my body until

I am aflame myself. You ask for my consent again. I hear myself reply 'Yes. I hand myself over to your will'. I break open further with each small step of surrender. The knife is at my throat, between my breasts, running around my vulva quickly covered in my juices. Your knife is at my lips and I kiss it.

You reach the agreed-upon spot and I open myself further to the Gods, you and my Master, willing myself open, relaxed. I surrender as you make the first cut, the sharp pain almost causes me to pass out. The smell of my blood both intoxicating and petrifying. I beg to come with the second cut, sure that I will not be able to contain the energy. 'Wait' you growl and I hold tight as the rest of the sigil is drawn. 'Now come' and I let go, wailing with the power.

Your hand is at my pussy. The lube is cool as you coat me well. My knees are up to ease opening. Three fingers in and I am concentrating, working hard to open to you. Banishing my fear of tearing, bearing down to give you more space. I am light-headed when you finally have your hand inside me and begin to make a fist. The fullness is so hot and also so uncomfortable. I want this and I don't want this and all I can do is moan, scream as you fuck me. I have never come like this in the past but I can feel myself so close. You push in deeper and I gush over your fist, squirting, coming, screaming until you decide I am finished.

I lie with you by the fire, languorous, replete.

9

I Miss You

Driving in my car on the country roads, music blasting from the BOSE speakers, tears coursing down my face for the tenth time today.

Grief overflowing again. I miss you.

Every moment of every day we are apart, I miss you.

My flesh stretched to breaking point trying to reunite with your flesh,

Trying to recreate whole.

I miss you, throat raw from sobbing, nail marks in my thighs from holding so tight to myself,

Trying so hard not to harm this flesh you own as I know you would not approve.

Heat flickering at my base... I can feel you blow on it until flames ignite

Fervid feverish sleep only to wake covered in my own sweat, my own hot oil

Overwhelming desire to scratch myself raw as though I could somehow rid my body of your mark

You live inside of me

Under my skin, in my bloodstream, in my neurons, your energy travelling between my synapses

Your touch

Your Will

Mould me

Your treasure

Your bitch

Your toy

Your slave

Yours

Just Yours

I think at your pleasure

I move at your pleasure

I exist as a separate being by your Will and at your pleasure

And so then how can I miss you

You, who are so much a part of me

How can I miss you when you are always here with me?

In my heart, my mind, under my skin, in my soul

Singeing my spirit

I do miss you.

I miss your flesh in contact with mine

I miss your scent on my tongue, my fingers, lingering on my clothes

I miss your taste

I miss your smile

Your eyes, particularly when they are hooded and filled with fire

I miss the curve of your nose

The texture of the skin on your stomach

The roughness of your ashy hands at the end of a day

Your whiskers on my thighs

I miss the oils from your scalp on my fingers – that I secretly smell for hours

I miss your soft lips, sweet tongue exploring my mouth

I miss your lips hard as you take my mouth when passion burns out of control

The feel of your hands in my hair, teeth on my throat

I miss the feel of your hair under my hands as I grab your head and pull you deeper into me at breakfast time

I miss you

The smell of your sweaty balls – salty tang on my tongue, inhaled makes me high

I miss you

The feel of your dick, half hard under my fingers

The feel of your dick rock hard pushing into my wet folds

I miss you

The taste of your throat… your skin under my fingers as I scratch you – moaning as you thrust into me

The feel of your hands as you drum on my ass

My thighs

My breasts

I miss you

Even the flick of those nasty damn fingers on my nipples

I miss the sound of Your voices in my ears

The sound of your heart beating as I lay my head on Your chest

I miss the sound of your laughter

The sight of your tears

I miss you

The stories you tell

The energy you weave

The love you pour over me

Every moment of every day we are apart

Each millisecond of separation

I miss you

Your smith's arms wrapped round me, crushing me to you as you kiss me

Letting me know

You miss me.

10

On the Train

The party is fairly boring. Lots of insipid guys talking politics with an air of superiority and trying hard to pull. I drink more than I intend so am tipsy by the time Dana and I head to the train home. Arms entwined, we wander to the back of the train where it is empty but for a lone hot man.

He's swarthy with deep hazel eyes, full lips a somewhat beak-like nose, and thick, dark, wavy hair. He has a cleft and a dimple. 'Oh yum. I would love some of that.' I whisper to Dana and she giggles. He looks over at us, his face turning a deep shade of red. 'I guess he heard me' I laugh. Intoxicated, whispering is beyond me.

Dana's hand slides down to my ass and between my cheeks. She teases me as she watches the man. She leads me over to the seat across from him and we sit down. We both went commando tonight and we are both wearing short dresses. As we sit we spread our legs wide so he has a perfect view of our bare glistening pussies. Dana tweaks my nipples until they are granite poking through my bra and my dress. I lean over and nibble at her ear before pulling her into a kiss.

I slowly suck her top lip between mine, nibbling and sucking until she moans. I look over at him and I can see his dick hard outlined hard in his pants. He is rubbing his hand over it. I am hungry. He reaches to touch us and Dana says 'not yet. Show us how you stroke your dick. We want to see it.' As she talks, she slides two fingers into my soaked cunt and uses her thumb to rub my clit. It slides under her thumb, a lubricated pearl in an oyster. I bite my lip to remain quiet. We don't want the guards to come back here and see what we are doing.

He slides his thick cock out of his pants and begins to stroke. He lowers his pants enough to get his balls out too – big and hairy. I start to drool as I watch him start to stroke. He slides his hand up to the head of his dick and squeezes. As he strokes, Dana continues to manipulate my pearl until I cannot hold it anymore. I come the first time as I watch the precum begin to bead on the head of his dick. He strokes more quickly and just before he is about to come, Dana grabs his hand to stop him.

'No don't come yet. I want to sit on your cock.' She lifts her dress and slides down on him – her back facing him . I kiss her deeply as she begins to ride his cock. She tastes like the sweet champagne we had been drinking. I suck on her tongue in time to her thrusts onto his cock. The sound of her soaked cunt sliding up and down on his cock makes me crazy. I suck on her tongue, exploding for a second time as I do.

I lean down to suck Dana's nipples, bringing a hand to her clitoris as she rides the man whose name we still don't know. Her skin is flushed all over a deep pink hue. Her nipples are like pink sapphires. Her sweat is slightly salty. Dana's small breast fills my mouth. I hum as I suck on her, the vibration causing her to giggle and then moan. My teeth scrape over her nipple causing a gasp. The man's fingers dig into Dana's hips as she rides him. He leans in and nibbles on her ears, then reaches around her, putting one hand in my hair and pulling me in closer.

I sit on the same bench, sliding my open legs around them both. I press into Dana, rubbing my overflowing cunt on her thigh as I do, working hard to make good contact and keep up the pressure because I want to come again. I increase the pressure on Dana's clitoris as she rides harder and faster until she explodes, soaking my fingers. Dana slides off the man and pushes me towards him. 'Your turn to ride' she says. 'No' I say. 'I want to clean him off and suck him until he feeds me. I lower my head to start licking his cock clean. My ass is in the air as lap Dana's juices and his precum of his dick. The movement of the train feels so good.

Dana slides a finger into my pussy and another into my ass and begins to fuck me hard and fast. I suck the man's cock into my mouth and then throat – taking as much of him as I can into my throat. He is so thick, he strains my mouth. The fullness feels so good. His hands are in my hair, gripping, pulling. He uses my hair to push more deeply into my throat until he is controlling my breathing with his thrusts. Dana fucks me in rhythm while with her other hand she fucks herself.

I can feel the man getting closer. I move from sucking his cock to trying to suck in both his balls. I love the raspy feel of his wiry pubic hair on my tongue. I use my lips to pull on his ball sack and run my tongue between his balls. His hands are still buried in my hair. He and Dana are kissing and he is moaning into his mouth. Dana is still fucking my cunt and my ass. The rocking of the train now is increasing our rhythm. He pulls my head up to his cock and shoves himself into my throat an instant before he comes. His semen is thick and salty-sweet and as the taste of it hits my tongue, I squirt soaking Dana's hand, dress, and the seat.

'While you are down there, my pussy needs licking' Dana says, her tone brooking no challenge. I move to lick her – long strokes, gathering up her sticky sweet juice. I lick the length of her pussy a few times before she grabs my head to direct me to her clitoris. Her clit is so different from mine. Mine is small and hooded. Hers is big – over an inch and a half long – and thick. I suck her into my mouth, licking around the head of her clit as though it were a small dick. I work her clit as she moans. She holds my head to her pussy – pressing into my mouth, barely letting me up for a breath. She rides my tongue, my face as she moves toward another orgasm. The train rhythm helps her as she gets closer and closer until she explodes. I swallow her delicious juice.

The three of us take some time to catch our breath. Dana and I arrange our clothing and get ready to exit the train at the next stop. The man is still sitting with his cock out. We hear the guard coming and throw a coat over his lap. We dissolve into laughter after the guard passes. We both kiss the man goodbye. He asks for our details and we just shake our heads and kiss him again. We bounce off the train at the next stop.

The scent of the man and Dana mingle on my face. I can smell them both and it makes me want to fuck Dana right there in the street. We barely get in the door to my house before I push her against the wall, my knee between her legs pressing on her clitoris until she moans. Dana pushes me back and we end up wrestling on the floor.

Dana wins and slides down my body, kissing, licking, and nipping at me as she goes. She sucks at my labia and dives between to grab my hard clit between her teeth. I shiver and hope to avoid her biting. She begins to suck and lick in earnest until I am screaming in pleasure. She starts rubbing on my G – spot as she continues to suck and lick until I bathe her face in my fluids. We lie on the floor panting. When her breathing returns to normal, Dana pads off to the loo to clean up. I don't move from the floor until she returns. She is already dressed. 'I have to get home – early start in the morning.' She leans down and kisses me. 'Drive safe.' I say. I drag myself up and see her out, then head off to the bathroom to clean up before slipping between the sheets.

11

Warm Morning

Warm morning
Vines enfolded
Time stops somehow
Simply can't talk
Gathering the fire
Dagger pierces her without breaking
Reality trembles between the future veil
Escapes the edge burning
Tears shine as they fall
Today's colour raven blaze
Sanguine drops shine as they fall
Warm morning
Sun streaks rainbows on smoked glass panes

Jagged flame walks over each vertebra
From the coccyx to the base of the skull
Etching patterns in pale skin
Leaving behind the smell of burned flesh
Branded into her flesh
Cauterising wounds from the past
Marking her soul as Theirs

Warm morning
Arms snake around her waist at the window
Contrasting colours shadows and shades
Contrasting textures pleasure and pain
Speech still eludes her
Rooting into the earth
Beneath Their feet

12

Braids

'You would look great with cane rows' H mused as she played with my curls. 'I will take you to the sister that does my hair'. Once H decided I should have braids, that was it. 'I need permission!' I exclaimed. 'He'll give you permission.' She was absolutely sure that this would be forthcoming.

H was right. He thinks I will look great with braids. He loves the idea of seeing me like this so we make the appointment. The London shop is a really small one. Music plays, a DVD in Susu is on. People are talking and laughing. The movie is from Guinea and various people are making fun of it. The men are shouting at the film and laughing.

It doesn't take me long to figure out that there are at least three nationalities in this little shop without including me. Nigeria, Guinea, Ghana are all represented and there are a couple of British-born people there too. I am the only American and the only white-passing person there.

H comes with me and tells the hairdresser what it is that I want but then tells me she needs to leave. I had expected her to be there with me through at least some of the process but she is off dealing with family things. There are not many English speakers in the shop and this makes me really anxious.

Having my hair done is an intimate activity. The hair wash is always very intimate. I adore when a lover brushes, washes, and dries my hair. The braiding adds another level of intimacy. In order to make the braids near the roots, the stylist has to get very close.

The tight braids make me feel like I am being held. I can only compare this to the feeling I have when wearing a corset that is firmly laced rather than laced for training. It is a feeling of warmth and support that I associate with comfort.

The braids feel like a firmly tied corset. The tying at

the hair roots is painful but strangely reassuring. I am usually quite tender-headed but this does not feel as I expected it to feel. I'm not sure why. I hope that she didn't tie the braids too tightly as I don't want a headache.

I am in the chair for five hours as she braids. After a while, I settle into a comfortable space, observing what is going on around me, relaxed as I do. She tugs my hair and then quickly braids. Each pull and tug also tugs at my pussy. I smell my juice seep out from my WAP. Wet Ass Pussy is what I have while this woman pulls, tugs, pushes at my hair. She smells delicious – of amber and vanilla and sugar. She leans over and her breasts are almost touching my nose. I inhale and begin to salivate. I catch myself before I lick her breast. Her nipples press against my arm as she leans in close again.

I love the tone of her voice. I cannot understand a word she is saying as she speaks to her friends and her colleagues in the shop. She speaks in three languages while I am there including English. Her banter with the men in the shop is intense. I can only imagine what she is saying. They all laugh throughout the conversation.

A tall fine deep dark man with a delicious bass voice is talking about me but I have no idea what he is saying. I think he is asking who I am and I wonder how the stylist is explaining me. I hear her mention H. He laughs and it is one of those deep raucous laughs that starts in the belly. My nipples harden in response to him. She leans in again and presses into my breasts. She must be able to feel how hard they are but she doesn't let on and just continues to braid.

By the time the stylist is finished, I am stuck to my panties. I have covered myself with sweet sticky pussy juice thinking about what it would be like to be tasting her pussy, licking it, sucking her clit, and burying my face in her vulva so that I am covered with her sweet juice. Her musk makes me drip. I am lost in my fantasy and it takes her three times to get my attention. I flush a deep crimson and she laughs. Then she says something and the men and one other woman laugh too. I am sure that they all know what I was daydreaming about.

When I pay, she doesn't let go of my hand. She looks into my eyes directly and licks her luscious pillowy lips. I realise I am staring. She grabs my hand and pulls me in close, stroking my face, and my arm. Bringing her lips so close to mine but not quite touching. The men and women are egging her on in the background. Her breath is on my lips. I open my mouth – inhaling deeply, tasting her breath at the same time that I smell it. Sweet breath. So heady that I am about to fall to my knees.

And then I remember where I am: in public. In a small hair salon. She reaches out and grabs me around the waist. In full view of everyone, she pulls me in for a kiss. Her lips take my mouth – she sucks, nibbles, tastes, licks. I can only receive. My arms go around her as she pulls me in closer, licking my teeth, tongue, sucking my tongue in. The kissing goes on for ages. Her breasts are pressed into mine – our hard nipples rubbing together. I want to push my pussy into hers. To rub against her mound until I explode. But there are people here.

She doesn't care. She pulls me into position against a wall, spreads my thighs with her thigh, and rubs her pussy over my knee and up my thigh. I feel her juices through her pants and smell her musk moaning. My lips are at her ear begging 'please please let me taste you. So hungry. Please I just want to taste'. She chuckles and pushes me to my knees. She pushes my head up under her dress pulls me in until I am sandwiched between her strong brown thighs. They are mottled and thick like tree trunks. Her laugh is almost a cackle as she closes her thighs on my head and squeezes until I feel like my head will burst open like a melon. 'Eat me well girl or I will break your head open' she says and laughs uproariously. Her panties are soaked and I suck on them for a moment. I pull them down with my teeth as she bumps my face, squeezing her thighs around my ears and rocking her hips.

My hand is between my legs, my fingers playing on my clitoris as I get my first taste of her. I lap up her juice from the bottom of her vagina and her perineum up all the way to her clitoris. And then I begin to eat in earnest. Sucking on her clitoris, licking her clitoris, her vulva, gathering the juices from her vulva and vagina. Nibbling at her lips and sucking in her clitoris. She grabs my head as she moans and holds my head pressed into her – breathing is not possible as she grinds her pussy and clitoris into my face. I breathe at her pleasure.

The men have come closer. One takes my hand and puts it around his hard cock. I cannot get all the way around but I do what I can. He is stroking into my hand. His friend wraps my hair around his dick and starts stroking himself off with my hair. The braids that have taken 5 hours to create are coming undone. I cannot complain. This is so hot. He strokes and strokes, braids wrapped tight. She holds me tight to her pussy and comes, squirting and filling my mouth with her ejaculate. She fills my mouth over and over again as she keeps coming and keeps squirting.

She finishes and strokes my face as she moves my head back from her pussy. 'You thirsty?' she asks and winks, then pulls me back in and fills my mouth and throat with hot piss. I swallow quickly as my clitoris pulses and my orgasm begins. She fills my throat over and over with her hot piss and then turns and pulls my head in between her ass cheeks. My tongue is tickling her asshole when she bears down and swallows my tongue. I fuck her asshole with my tongue until she is screaming in pleasure. By the time she finishes, my tongue is sore.

She turns my face to the man who is wanking with my hair. 'Shoot in her face' she shouts and all it takes is one more pull and he explodes streaking my face in his hot sticky jizz. He wipes himself off over my lips and tells me to open. His semi-hard dick pushes into my mouth. 'Thirsty?' he laughs and fills my throat with piss. His piss is so much more acrid than hers.

He laughs as I gulp and gulp. His friend pushes him. 'My turn' as he strokes his cock faster. The first of his come hits my face within a second of his friend moving away from my face. He brings his balls to my lips and jerks his dick off on top of my head as I am sucking his balls. His come sprays into my hair and drips down from the crown of my head. I keep coming over and over as they amuse themselves with me.

There are two more women in the shop who have been watching. 'Ay,' one says 'bring her mouth over here.' The stylist pushes me towards her until my lips are at her friend's wet cunt. She smells strong and somehow that makes me even hotter. I dive in licking, sucking, and soon she is riding my face and making yipping sounds as she comes, soaking me. Her other friend pushes me onto my back on the floor. She is a BBW and spreads her big, beautiful ass cheeks as she lowers herself onto my face. I begin to lick her asshole and she bears down. 'Deeper' she moans and bears down hard. The pressure on my face is intense. She pulses her asshole. Bearing down as I feast on her asshole. She comes with my tongue deep inside her asshole. She slides forward and fills my mouth with piss. 'Yes, girl yes. You drink.

That is my nectar. You lucky I don't feed you my caviar.' She cackles and everyone laughs. I come as she finishes filling my throat. 'You tink about that white girl' she laughs. 'Yes, you come when you tink about me feeding you'.

The stylist takes me to clean up and then re-fixes my hair. 'Come back again' she says as I get ready to leave. I keep my braids in for 6 weeks and the whole time I dream about the next time I have a reason to return to that shop.

13

On Your Knees

'On your knees', he growls as he enters the room. I lay curled up on a thick crimson silk blanket. I rise to my knees quickly, thighs open, palms open face up on my thighs, chin up, eyes lowered, mop of copper curls in disarray from sleep. My heart is pounding, the blood rushing in my ears. I smell his anger and his arousal – pungent musk with an acrid tang. The after-taste of tobacco arouses me unexpectedly. I always associate that taste and smell with him. It has been 10 years since I smoked a cigarette and I still crave them at times of stress, when I am angry and when someone smokes around me – particularly at the end of a good meal. I don't dare smoke again. My doctors have told me it would make my autoimmune disease worse and my owner just said 'no' in the voice that doesn't allow any negotiation.

With effort, I keep my eyes down. Without restraints, without commands, I struggle inside to keep to my place. I bite my tongue to stop myself from speaking. He chuckles. 'That's right. Be quiet. Just wait.' His deep voice sends ripples of pleasure through me. I can smell my own arousal which just causes it to swell and my cunt to swell too.

I moan. The waiting is filled with energy, attention paid to every sight, every sound, each nuance, the kinetics of arousal. My heat rises. The charge builds in me until I am sure I will become lightning during a volcanic eruption. His hand grasps a handful of the soft coils, twists them around his wrist, and pulls my head back until he can look into my eyes. I know better than to try to avoid his gaze but I allow my eyes to close as I feel the tug on the base of my skull and I purr with desire.

'What is your name?' He demands. 'E' I reply. The slap catches me unprepared. My head snaps back with force and tears spring to my eyes. He traces his handprint as I shudder, one tear sliding down my cheek.

'What is your name?' He growls. I tremble and whisper 'E'. He pulls my head back further. My neck stretches taut as violin strings. He strokes the bone-chilling metal of the gun barrel against my cheek. Tears spill down my face. He strokes the muzzle of the gun over my neck. The smell of the gun oil mixes with the sour smell of my fear. He asks me one more time. 'What is your name?'. 'I have no name' I whisper.

He removes his belt. It is black leather and made to wear with jeans and work clothing, not a suit. I smell saddle soap and oils as he strokes my face with it. He wraps it round his fist. I struggle to remain quiet but cannot suppress a deep moan. The sound moves through my whole body, in waves. He presents the belt, wrapped round his fist for me to my mouth. I kiss the belt and taste the flesh side – salty with a tang. I imagine the taste and texture of my blood, viscous and metallic.

He bends me over the bench. I hear the whoosh of the belt just before it welts my ass. I yelp but do not move. He hits me four times quickly – each stripe landing slightly higher than the last. My whole ass is burning. I can feel the welts beginning to rise. The next four stripes come more violent on top of the first four. I scream, still managing to hold myself in place. My flesh is on fire. My cunt is seeping juice onto my thighs and the bench. My nipples are like rubies – hard and red.

In one smooth stroke, He enters my slick pussy, pressing hard cock so deep I can feel him in my chest. He has one hand in my hair, pulling my head back, exposing my throat as he thrusts into me. He pounds into my raw ass, bending me into a bow. I howl my pain and my pleasure. He lets go my hair and rakes claws down my back, down my arms as he continues to fuck me. He is bent over me, fucking me harder and faster. He growls in my ear 'Come'. I howl my release as he bites into my neck. He thrusts again, grabbing my breasts, raking over my nipples with claws, pulling me to him as he empties his balls deep inside his pussy. He collapses on top of me, pressing my body into the bench, pressure on my raw bruised flesh. 'Mine' he growls into my ear, biting hard enough to draw blood. He gathers the tears from my face as he murmurs 'mine'.

14

Edges

I have always enjoyed the burn. This one sits at my solar plexus and spreads out to every part of my body. The burn bears the scent and taste of you. Can you hear my begging over the energy wave?

I have never been the most patient of people. When I hunger, I want it now. When I connect, I want to immerse myself in the connection. As I have gotten older and gained more experience, I have learned to temper that to immerse myself for a time daily or a time weekly – whatever the relationship demands. But when the energy tastes so sweet, my desire rages.

I love feeling energy pushed into me and equally,

I love feeling it pulled from me. That feeling that makes me weak – the desire that finds me saying 'take more please take more' – the heaviness and lightness. I find it so difficult to describe. Those who understand, do so. Others – well explaining will be someone else's job. I find myself lost for words.

I love edges. I have always known that about myself and I have continued to embrace this love more and moreover the past years. I love that liminal place just as much – I love to be the bridge – or step into/out of /over that place. Dip my toe into the fog in between.

I fear that I will fall and get lost in that liminal place and yet, I know that I will not. My anchors to this world remain strong. I enjoy what my body can do for me and for others and don't seek to shed it just yet.

As I write, my mouth fills with saliva – I am aching to taste you. I have always been so oral. Smell and taste have such an intense impact upon me. Voices as well. Kinaesthetic equal to voices/sounds. Visual has the least impact upon me.

The landscape changes in front of me and I find myself back in the forest. I can smell the sea so I must not be too far from the coast. The sea scent mixes with the scents of the trees and wood smoke. The darkness lit only by the fire. I can hear the chuntering and grumbles of animals in the wood surrounding me. The hair rises on the back of my neck, goosebumps on my naked body. And in my head, I hear 'Something wicked this way comes' followed by laughter and then 'well sadistic more than wicked'. This sets me to trembling.

Nails run over my back or are they claws? I almost scream as I did not hear you approach. My hearing is compromised and I wonder if it is because I don't have hearing aids in or because you are an accomplished predator. With effort, I hold my position. I don't want to disappoint. The edge of a blade seeks entry. I spread my thighs wider, slow my breathing. Try to still my absolute panic as I feel the tip push into my nether lips. You chuckle noting my every response.

You move closer behind me, press into me so there is as little space between our bodies as possible. Your knife is at my throat and then on the pinna of my left ear. 'I am going to pierce you here'. You say very matter-of-factly. My panic rises. Piercings have never settled well but then I have never had a ritual piercing. Piercings have always been, well, decorative. And my body has not co-operated. This is decidedly different.

'Not yet' you say as I struggle to hold myself still. 'But soon'. I am conflicted. 'Surrender' I tell myself. I work to manage my desire to control any part of this connection and simply surrender.

15

Wings

I wake with the fire alive and running up my spine. It starts at the base, swirling around all dark blue peaks, the most intense heat. It melts my pussy and the lava begins to flow from between my legs.

The flames rise up to my solar plexus where they are red, orange, tipped with yellow. They spread throughout my body. My breasts are heavy with them, nipples larger, darker even when soft. My throat opens and the flames burn through. Up to my neck that cracks as I turn my head and stretch my shoulders back.

The pain is incidental as my wings break through

– released unfurling as I stretch. My nipples harden until they are like rubies – red-brown hard. I rise on the flames – tentatively. I fly on the edge of the flame to meet you.

You wrap your wings around me, sink your teeth into my shoulder and I bellow out a roar in protest that quickly turns to pleasure. You slick yourself in the lava flowing from my pussy and push into my ass. I moan at the feel of you pulsing white-hot inside me – moving to meet your thrusts – craving more, harder please – the hurt causing my juices to flow more thickly. Fire pouring from my mouth, my throat as I roar again.

You bend me back around the throat, controlling my breathing as you pace your thrusts – slowly sliding in and out of my ass – plunging deep, stroking shallow – the pace building slowly as I beg to come, beg to be allowed to let go. You push deeper, harder until I cannot stop – orgasm starting at the bottom of my spine – fire rushing through me to the top of my head and then back to the base of my spine – circling three, four, five times before I go limp with pleasure.

You haven't finished and pick up the pace again – pounding into my ass. I can do naught but receive your thrusts and breathe at your pleasure. You explode into my ass – melting my insides – until my body dissolves into pure light. Minutes later/hours later (time is irrelevant) I settle slowly back into my human form. Overcome by the delicious languor from the heat – almost too hot – on the edge of burning – I drift until I drift into sleep.

16

Epilogue

I am happiest when I am able to write each day, but my life doesn't always allow for that. When things get too busy for me to carve out time, I look forward to my quarterly writing retreats. Usually, I go away to write. It removes me from the routine and makes it easier for me to ignore the myriad distractions that arise each and every day because I run my own business, have two dogs, a young adult son & a husband/Master to attend to.

In 2020/2021, going away for a retreat was difficult and then impossible. I have had to create a new routine around writing retreats that allow for me working at home. While I adjusted, I do look forward to being able to resume my retreats away from home. For now, I wish you joy, abundance, love, and lust from a village in Kent, United Kingdom.

Other Books by the Author

Bisbey & Bisbey, Brief Therapy for Post-Traumatic Stress Disorder: Traumatic Incident Reduction and Related Techniques, 1998, John Wiley & Sons.

Bisbey & Griffyn, Rites of Passage, 2001.

Bisbey, Lori Beth, Dancing the Edge to Surrender: An Erotic Memoir of Trauma & Survival, 2020, Dr Lori Beth Bisbey®

Bisbey, Lori Beth, Dancing the Edge to Reclaiming Your Reality: Essential Life Skills for Gaslighting (& Trauma) Survivors, 2021, Dr Lori Beth Bisbey®

Bisbey & Burnett (editors), Visibility: Success Stories from Elite Leaders Making an Impact from the Stage, 2021, Hybrid Global Publishing.

About the Author

Dr Lori Beth Bisbey is a clinical psychologist, author, speaker & a sex & intimacy coach. She has spent over 30 years helping people to create and sustain meaningful and exciting relationships with fantastic sex (without shame). She specialises in GSRD (gender, sexuality, relationship diversity), is consensual non-monogamy and kink BDSM knowledgable. She also specialises in helping traumatised people to move from victim to survivor and back into life.

Dr Bisbey hosts a weekly internet radio show, The A to Z of Sex® on the Health & Wellness Channel of Voiceamerica.com. She speaks at events, conferences and presents workshops worldwide. She has been writing erotica since she was a teenager.

Dr Bisbey identifies as a queer polyamorous leather woman. Her pronouns are she/her.

For more information https://drloribethbisbey.press

Printed in Great Britain
by Amazon

78739105R00089